It was like w...
dance of se...

Admiration and something else I was much less familiar with moved through me and settled into a hot little pool in my center. Then the man's hands were on the horse, moving gently over it while he continued to croon, quieting the animal. I had no idea how long I sat there, watching man and horse.

And imagining what it would feel like to have those hands on me.

Realizing what I was doing, I started to get up. But I'd forgotten about my ankle, and when I put my full weight on it, I sat right back down with a little squeal.

He turned to me. "You're hurt. Did one of his hooves..." His voice trailed off and his eyes narrowed. "Cameron? I didn't recognize you...."

Of course he hadn't. My sister Cameron was missing. I hadn't recognized him either. He'd been intent on calming the horse...and I'd been equally intent on watching him. It was only now, as he tethered his stallion and strode toward me, that I realized that this was Sloan Campbell.

My sister's fiancé.

Dear Reader,

Until a few weeks ago, Brooke Ashby has lived all her adventures vicariously through the exciting story lines she creates for the popular soap opera *Secrets*. But when she suddenly learns that she's adopted and that she has an identical twin sister—the heiress to the McKenzie horse ranch—who's mysteriously gone missing, Brooke decides to take the stage in a real-life story line. Her plan is to appear at the ranch posing as her twin and to solve the mystery of her sister's disappearance.

Of course, the problems in any story line are the plot twists. First of all, the *secrets* at the ranch rival anything she's ever written for her soap. Then there's her surprising and uncontrollable attraction to Sloan Campbell, her sister's handsome and enigmatic fiancé, who may be responsible for her sister's disappearance—and who isn't buying in to her masquerade. She should avoid him at all costs. But how can she when he may be the only one who can lead her to her sister?

Then someone tries to kill her!

I hope you love Gothic mysteries as much as I do, and I hope you'll join Brooke and Sloan as they uncover all the *secrets* and discover love. I love to hear from my readers. Visit my Web site—www.carasummers.com—and let me know what you think.

Happy reading!

Cara Summers

TELL ME
YOUR SECRETS...
Cara Summers

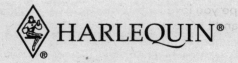

HARLEQUIN®

TORONTO • NEW YORK • LONDON
AMSTERDAM • PARIS • SYDNEY • HAMBURG
STOCKHOLM • ATHENS • TOKYO • MILAN • MADRID
PRAGUE • WARSAW • BUDAPEST • AUCKLAND

ISBN-13: 978-0-373-79290-0
ISBN-10:   0-373-79290-5

TELL ME YOUR SECRETS...

This edition published by arrangement with Harlequin Books S.A.

® and TM are trademarks of the publisher. Trademarks indicated with ® are registered in the United States Patent and Trademark Office, the Canadian Trade Marks Office and in other countries.

www.eHarlequin.com

Printed in U.S.A.

ABOUT THE AUTHOR

Since making her first sale, Cara Summers has written twenty-two books for the Harlequin Duets, Temptation and Blaze lines. When she was asked if she'd like to write a sexy Gothic mystery for the Blaze line, she jumped at the chance. According to Cara, "The first romances I ever read were Gothic novels—*Jane Eyre*, *Wuthering Heights*, *Rebecca*, *Nine Coaches Waiting*. If it weren't for the fact that I fell in love with those stories, I might never have become a romance writer." Her next books for the line will be a trilogy released in 2007 about three (very sexy) Greek brothers—Kit, Nik and Theo Angelis—who are Tall, Dark and... You get the picture!

Books by Cara Summers

To my newest daughter-in-law-to-be, Gert Fulmer.
Thank you for the love and joy that you bring to
my son, Kevin, and to our whole family.
(And thanks for being a fan and
enjoying my stories!)

1

"I CAN'T MAKE UP MY MIND. Shall I have the scones with clotted cream—and ooooh, look at those strawberries...but the triple-chocolate layer cake is calling my name."

My friend Pepper Rossi was studying the three-tiered dessert caddie the waitress had just delivered as if the fate of the world depended on her decision.

I felt equally serious about the decision that I had made. After plotting and planning for the last three days, I'd come to San Francisco to run it by Pepper.

Nerves knotted in my stomach. But I managed to keep my hand steady as I lifted the silver teapot and filled Pepper's cup and then my own. I'd always run my plans by her when we were roommates in college.

Of course, those days were well behind us now that we were established career women. I had a job as a writer for a successful Los Angeles based soap opera, *Secrets*, and Pepper worked as a P.I. at Rossi Investigations, her brothers' up-and-coming security firm in San Francisco. Recently, she'd met the man of her dreams, Cole Buchanan, an ex-CIA agent who also worked for her brothers. From the glow on her face whenever she mentioned him, it was a match made in heaven.

Even more recently than that, I'd engaged Pepper in her professional capacity to do a job for me. Hiring a P.I. was a first for me. But then life was throwing me one surprise after another lately.

Pepper's hand was still hovering over the dessert caddie. "Take the cake," I urged her. "You know you're not going to be able to resist it." Pepper was a fellow chocoholic.

"You're sure?" she asked.

"If it's as good as it looks, we'll ask the waitress to bring another."

There was a time when indulging in chocolate had gone a long way toward helping me to deal with life's ups and downs. But it had lost some of its therapeutic value since the day five weeks ago when my whole world had shifted on its axis. That's when I'd received an anonymous letter telling me that I was adopted.

Up until that moment, I'd led a rather uneventful existence—if you discount the broken collarbone I'd suffered at age eleven when my horse Dandelion's Pride and I had parted company during a jump. I'd believed my parents were John and Marsha Ashby, both successful neurosurgeons in Chicago.

I was sure the letter was a prank, but my curiosity had kicked in and I'd phoned my parents. Mom and Dad had both gotten on the line in one of our typical "conference" calls. As busy and dedicated doctors, they'd always thought it more time efficient if they talked to me together. When I'd told them about the letter, I'd expected them to laugh and deny it, to reassure me that I was indeed their biological daughter and then get back to their busy lives.

But they hadn't laughed and they hadn't denied it. Instead, there'd been this long silence on the other end of the line. With my stomach clenched, I'd pushed for more information, and they'd finally confessed to the fact that they'd adopted me and they gave me the name of the private agency they'd used.

The moment I'd hung up I'd called Pepper and asked her to trace my biological family. A week ago, she'd sent me the information that had given me the first clue to my real past. She hadn't been able to locate my biological mother. Her search had dead-ended when she found the adoption papers for me—and my twin sister, who'd been raised as the only daughter of James and Elizabeth McKenzie on their horse ranch near San Diego.

My first rather giddy reaction when I'd received the news was that this would make a great story line for *Secrets*. Twins separated at birth. My head writer was going to love me. Mallory Carstairs, the bad-girl diva of the show, was currently in a coma, and now she could awake to find she had a twin sister....

Then I'd reined in my overactive imagination for a reality check. I wasn't a character on a soap opera. I was ordinary, nothing-ever-happens-to-me Brooke Ashby.

Except I had a twin sister I'd never met—an heiress who'd been missing for five weeks.

I watched Pepper slice into the chocolate cake. I'd let her enjoy one bite before I told her my plan. My head writer had been thrilled when I'd told her what I was going to do and she'd been more than willing to give me some time off. But I was sure that Pepper wasn't going to be equally happy with me.

I watched with envy as she savored that first bite.

Then as she scooped up a second, I took a fortifying sip of tea and said, "I'm going to the McKenzie ranch and masquerade as my sister."

The cake froze just inches from Pepper's open mouth, before her fork dropped with a clatter. "You're *what?*"

Pepper's voice was loud enough to make the elegantly dressed lady at a nearby table aim a frown in our direction. High tea at the sedate St. Francis Hotel in San Francisco was not the place for loud voices.

I cleared my throat and spoke around the little bubble of panic that had lodged in my throat. "Don't worry. I've plotted it all out. I'm going to the McKenzie ranch posing as my twin sister, Cameron McKenzie."

"Your *missing* twin sister. Didn't you read the report I sent you? She disappeared five weeks ago. No one knows where she is."

I'd read the report over and over again, trying to glean every detail I could about my newly discovered twin. I tried a confident smile. "If she weren't missing, I wouldn't be able to take her place."

Pepper leaned forward, this time keeping her voice low. "Brooke, you can't be serious about this. Five weeks is a long time. If there was foul play involved in her disappearance, then you could be putting yourself in danger."

Pepper's words had my stomach performing that little "flip" it had been doing ever since I'd first learned that my sister was missing. I set down my teacup. "I knew it. You *do* think something's happened to her, don't you?"

Pepper raised both hands. "I didn't say that. The family hasn't filed a missing persons report. They say she's gone off like this before in a temper or on a whim. They claim not to be concerned."

Wedding jitters was the official story that the family had put out. Always a bit headstrong, Cameron had simply gone away to "settle her nerves" about her upcoming wedding to Sloan Campbell. According to what Pepper had discovered, Sloan Campbell, the orphaned son of a man who'd once run the McKenzie stables, had been raised on the ranch but had left five years earlier to make his own fortune in the world as a horse trainer. He'd been quite successful, too. In May, one of his horses had won the Kentucky Derby. That was where he and Cameron had run into one another again, and it had apparently been love at second sight. One of the press clippings had termed it a "perfect match" for McKenzie Enterprises. Sloan was the expert when it came to horses, and Cameron was proving to be very talented at bringing in new business.

I drew out the report that Pepper had sent me and placed it on the table between us. I had lots of questions about the marriage and about Sloan Campbell. When someone disappears, it's always the husband or the fiancé who's the prime suspect.

"When Sloan marries Cameron—*if* the wedding actually takes place next month—they jointly inherit both the McKenzie land and the business." The business being a multimillion-dollar horse breeding and training facility that James McKenzie and his father and grandfather before him had established and built. "Why jointly? Why not leave the whole thing to his only daughter?"

"My thought exactly," Pepper said. "So I checked into it and discovered that James McKenzie is a patriarch in the true sense of the word. In spite of the fact that he's survived into the twenty-first century, he has the antiquated idea that a woman can't run the ranch on her own."

I tapped my finger on the report. "My sister sounds pretty competent."

"I agree. But the McKenzies seem to be a stubborn lot, and she hasn't been able to convince her father of that. And there may be more involved from a business standpoint. Bringing back Sloan Campbell was a real coup. After his horse won the Derby, he could have pretty much written his ticket in terms of job offers. But from what I've been able to dig up, he wasn't going to work for anyone else. He was going to use the nest egg he's been saving up for the past few years to buy a ranch and build his own business. That was probably his goal when he left and went out on his own five years ago. I'm figuring a deal where he gets half of the McKenzie Ranch—an already established place—was a powerful lure."

"But even if Cameron only comes into half the estate, there are millions involved and she's missing. Any way you look at it, there's a motive for foul play."

"Which is why I don't want you to go there pretending to be her," Pepper said. "If you're curious, why not just go as yourself?"

"I thought of that. But I'd just be a stranger. They could serve me tea and then brush me off."

Pepper reached over and took my hand in hers. "This is a sister you didn't even know existed until I sent you that report. If you're worried about her, Cole and I can look into this further."

"They don't have to talk to you, either. But if I go there posing as Cameron, there's no way they can brush me off. I'll have a chance to see things and learn things as an insider. And I have a plan all plotted out."

Pepper shook her head. "This isn't a story line for your soap opera. You know you have a tendency to leap into things before you look."

I took another fortifying sip of tea. My parents would have been in full agreement with her. As long as I could remember, I'd been cursed with an *Alice In Wonderland*–like curiosity. It was probably one of the reasons I became a writer. It wasn't that great a leap from wondering what's going to happen next to inventing what's going to happen next.

"I know I can pull it off. I've studied all the photographs you sent me in the file plus a few I've dug up on my own. From what I can see, Cameron and I are identical twins." We both had that Miranda from *Sex and the City* red hair. Of course, I wore mine in a braid down my back so I wouldn't have to fuss with it. Cameron, on the other hand, wore hers in one of those chic shoulder-length styles that I'd always admired.

"All I have to do is shorten my hair a bit," I assured Pepper. This was the part of the plan that was clear in my mind. I'd even made an appointment with a hairdresser.

"You're going to need more than a haircut to pull this off."

Exactly. That was why I had come to San Francisco. I was going to need more, and Pepper had the power to provide all of it. I just had to get her on my side. I wasn't worried, not really. Hadn't I been cocaptain of the debate team at the small private college Pepper and I had attended? The only problem was that Pepper had been the other cocaptain and her strength had always been rebuttal.

"I'll need a little help from you, of course. But I know that I can pass for her."

"For how long?" Pepper asked. "A few photos and the information I gave you won't be enough. Someone is bound to figure out you're a phony."

"I told you I have a plan."

"You always do." Pepper's frown deepened. "But sometimes they don't work out."

I could tell she was thinking of the time I had the great idea about slipping away from the dorm and going to a frat party at the neighboring state school. My plan had included donning disguises, climbing out of our dorm window via sheets we had knotted together, and "borrowing" our resident advisor's car. It would have worked if we hadn't had a flat tire and the local sheriff hadn't stopped to help us out.

Pepper squeezed my hand. "Look, I know that this has been a shock to you—first finding out that you're adopted and then learning that you have an identical twin."

This was another reason why I'd driven up to San Francisco to talk to Pepper. Yes, I needed her help, but I also needed someone besides my parents to talk to. Mom and Dad were busy. They'd always been busy. Not that they hadn't loved me and been proud of me. They had. But...

"What can I do to talk you out of this?"

I met her eyes steadily. "You can't. I don't believe that Cameron's disappearance is due to the fact that she needed time away to 'settle her nerves.' I have this feeling that something's wrong and that she needs my help."

Pepper's brows shot up. "A feeling? Are you talking about some special twin ESP?"

"Maybe."

She considered that for a moment and then said, "How does that work when you've never known each other, never even met?"

"How should I know? We came from the same egg, share the same genes. I'm figuring we have to be quite a bit alike." I paused to flip open the file that lay on the table between us. Pepper had been thorough in her research. She'd included pictures and background information on everyone at the McKenzie ranch. I pulled out a photo that had appeared in the local press announcing the engagement of Cameron McKenzie and Sloan Campbell. "Look at them. They look very happy together."

Pepper rolled her eyes. "They're posing for the press. They probably said 'cheese.'"

"Maybe." But I couldn't believe that what I saw in the photo was faked. It was the only picture that Pepper had included of my sister's fiancé, Sloan Campbell, and the same thing was happening to me that had happened every time I looked at it. I couldn't seem to take my eyes off of his face.

He was dark-haired and tall, nearly a full head and shoulders above Cameron. If she was wearing three-inch heels—and I figured from other photos she was—that meant he was over six feet tall. Even in a tux, it was apparent that his shoulders were broad. There was strength there, and a certain magnetism that would probably be even stronger when it wasn't being filtered through a camera lens. Hollywood and TV producers called it "star quality," and Sloan Campbell had it in spades.

Yet, he wasn't exactly handsome, at least not in a movie star pretty way. In my experience, actors built their muscles and hardened their abs in state-of-the-art health clubs. Sloan Campbell looked as if he kept in shape the old-fashioned way. He might not be movie star handsome, but there was something very compelling about his rugged features, something that made you believe that in a fight, this was the man you'd want on your side.

My instincts also told me that this was a man any red-blooded woman would want in her bed. I blinked as a thought struck me. Was this a man I wanted in my bed? Was that why I was so fascinated by his picture? I could feel heat flood my cheeks. He was my sister's fiancé. And they looked very happy.

"Earth to Brooke."

I dragged my eyes away from the newspaper clipping and met Pepper's again.

"I'm waiting for you to elaborate more on this 'feeling' of yours that your sister isn't a runaway bride."

"Okay." I drew in a deep breath. "From your accounts, Cameron loves the ranch and she holds an important job at McKenzie Enterprises. She gets to travel around the country, entertaining old clients and courting new ones. She's good at what she does, and the business depends on her. The other thing that's clear in your report is that she loves horses. That's one thing I share with her, and I don't think she would run away from her responsibilities. I think she'd handle her cold feet another way. She'd simply break off the engagement."

"Dammit." Pepper leaned back in her chair.

It was my turn to stare. "What's the matter?"

"You're beginning to make sense."

Before I could comment, a waitress appeared at our table.

"Can I get you something else?"

"Two glasses of your best Chardonnay," Pepper said. "I'm going to need more than chocolate to settle my nerves."

As soon as the waitress moved away, she leaned closer. "I've talked about this with Cole, and we tend to agree with you that Cameron wouldn't have run out on the job or the horses for this amount of time."

"Then you can understand why I have to go there."

Pepper grabbed my hand again. "What I see is a reason why you shouldn't go there. It's too dangerous. If someone else is responsible for your sister's disappearance, he or she is not going to be happy if you show up as Cameron. Plus, we still don't know who sent the anonymous letter—or why."

"You're not going to talk me out of this."

"Yeah," Pepper said as the waitress set down the glasses of wine. "That's why I ordered the drinks."

We reached for the wineglasses together and I raised mine in a toast. "To the best friend ever. Wish me luck?"

She touched her glass to mine and took a long swallow. "I have one more argument."

As cocaptain of the debate team, she'd always had one more argument.

"How in the world are you going to carry this masquerade off? All you know about your sister is in that file. And what about the fiancé? How do you intend to handle him?"

Very carefully, I thought. I had a good idea that Sloan Campbell would be my biggest challenge once I got to the ranch. Once more, I attempted a confident smile. "I've got it covered. I'm going to tell them that five weeks ago I got mugged, and when I woke up in the hospital, I didn't have any ID and couldn't remember who I was. That's why I haven't come back sooner. And that way I won't have to remember a thing about Cameron's past life."

Pepper sighed, then took a good gulp of her wine. "I should have known you'd come up with something. You always do."

I met her eyes steadily. "I have to do this. She's my sister. And I'm going to need your help."

"You bet your life you are." Pepper pulled out a notebook and began scribbling. "The mugging is a good idea. You arrived at the hospital with only the clothes on your back. So there was no way to trace you. We'll need to establish where you've been and what you've been doing for the last five weeks. You're a million-airess. Someone in the family is going to check into everything. And when the press gets hold of the story..."

She paused in her scribbling and tapped her pen on the notebook. "There will have to be a report about the mugging. Here in San Francisco, I think, because Luke has a friend who's a captain in the SFPD. Because of the amnesia, you won't have to explain why you were so far from home."

"I knew you'd know what to do," I said.

Pepper glanced up at me. "If you're determined to do this, I want your ass covered." Then she continued scribbling. "We'll also need a doctor who can verify the memory loss, a place where you've been staying the last few weeks, a job. Maybe when you came to Rossi Investigations to ask for our help, we gave you something temporary. We'll figure it out. Cole's really good at this sort of thing. And what he can't handle, my brother Luke can. He's magic when it comes to hacking into official records and tweaking them a bit."

I smiled at her. "This is just like *Charlie's Angels* with Charlie handling all the background cover stuff."

Pepper's brows shot up. "Except that Rossi Investigations is much better than Charlie Townsend any day."

"Of course, they are. That's why I hired your firm to help me find out who I was."

Pepper frowned at me. "And it took us five weeks to do the job?" Then she grinned. "Just kidding. Let them think we're some kind of hick agency. Plus, your mugging took place in San Francisco, and Cameron's disappearance didn't even make the papers around here." Her grin faded. "A definite sign of the power of the family to keep a lid on the story. You're going to have to be very careful."

"I will. Thanks for understanding."

Pepper leaned closer. "I know what it's like to find family that you didn't know existed. But once you get to the ranch, I want you to keep in daily contact with me. Cole has a plane. We can be there in less than an hour."

She set her pen down, and took a sip of her wine. "Once you get to the ranch, what's the rest of your plan?"

"You always ask the tough questions."

Pepper's eyes narrowed. "That's what friends are for."

I shrugged and took a good gulp of wine myself. "Once I get inside the hacienda, I'm going to play it by ear. I'm sure something will come to me. My best plots always come to me on the fly."

2

"WE'RE ALMOST THERE," Cole Buchanan said as he turned his sporty red convertible onto the winding road that led to the McKenzie ranch. He and Pepper had decided that Cole should bring me to the ranch, get the lay of the land, and test the atmosphere before he left. He would explain about my memory loss, the investigative work that Rossi Investigations had done to help me find out my true identity, and that way everyone at the ranch would know that there was someone on the outside that I could turn to for help—just in case.

Cole was my driver instead of Pepper because the Rossis had decided he had a bigger intimidation quotient than Pepper did. It was really no contest. At over six feet, with a rangy body that was pretty much all muscle, Cole was not someone you would want to go up against. I'd also learned that he'd done sniper work for the CIA.

The idea that he and Pepper had met, fallen in love and were making a match of it, would never have occurred to me—not even as a remote possibility. But I'd seen them together and they suited each other perfectly. I'd already been thinking of how I could adapt their story for *Secrets*. While looking for her long lost twin, Mallory Carstairs meets and hires an ex-sniper to help her out.

"You can always change your mind."

I jerked my thoughts back to the present.

"You don't have to stay at the ranch," Cole continued. "We can just say that you've hired me to make some inquiries and that you don't feel comfortable staying there until you find out why you ran away."

"No. I'll be fine." The whole idea of my coming to the ranch was to investigate Cameron's disappearance from the inside. "I'm just having a little attack of stage fright."

Truth told, I was having a major attack. Now that I was about to step out on stage, I was suddenly realizing that acting out story lines was a lot different than sitting on the sidelines and writing them. One of the things that I'd discovered in the past few days as I'd been poring over everything I could find about my sister was that we were different in one aspect. She would never have suffered from an attack of cold feet. Cameron had always been in a sort of limelight. Plus, she was confident, outgoing and probably very assertive. I, on the other hand, was a writer. While I experienced life vicariously through the characters I created, she went out there and boldly lived. I envied her that.

"We could also go to plan B and I could stay on as your bodyguard," Cole said.

That, too, was something we'd discussed during the three days I'd spent in the offices of Rossi Investigations while Pepper and Cole established my cover story and drilled into me every fact they'd dug up on the cast of characters at the ranch.

At the end of three days, I knew each one of the

players as well as I knew the characters on *Secrets*, maybe even better. But I'd rejected plan B. How was I supposed to find out anything with Rossi Investigation's biggest intimidation factor dogging my every step?

I turned to Cole and put on my most confident smile. "I'm going to be able to do this."

He pulled to a stop in front of an opened wrought iron gate that bore the name McKenzie Ranch. Then he turned to me. "I don't doubt that. Pepper has told me a lot about you. But if you want help, Pepper and I are a phone call away."

I felt tears prick behind my eyes. "Thanks. But I think I have a better chance of learning something if I do this alone. My sister would be able to do this. If I'm anything at all like her, I can, too."

Cole gave me a brief nod, then guided his car through the gate and up the winding driveway. When we rounded the last curve and the hacienda came into view, I gave a little gasp.

The Hacienda Montega was listed in every book that chronicled historic homes in California. In addition to being an excellent example of Spanish architecture, the house had a mysterious and colorful history. I'd done some research on it that went beyond Pepper's report. What I'd discovered was that the mistresses of the hacienda had a tendency to die young. Not even Cameron's father's wives had escaped. James McKenzie's first wife, Sarah, hadn't died, but she'd still been young when she'd run away with Sloan Campbell's father. Of course, I'd tucked that little piece of information away for a possible story line. Then James's second wife, Elizabeth, had passed away shortly after they'd adopted Cameron.

But there was a lighter and even more colorful side to the history, too. Originally built by Don Roberto Montega on the occasion of his marriage to the Spanish Countess Maria Francesca in the eighteenth century, the hacienda had eventually fallen into the hands of a silent film producer who'd only owned it a year before he'd lost both the hacienda and the land to a professional gambler named Silas McKenzie.

And the rest was history, as they say. Silas had married, mended his gambling ways and turned to his first love, raising Thoroughbred horses. From the looks of the hacienda, the stables and the other outbuildings, he must have had a knack for it. James, the current owner of the estate, was his grandson.

All of the pictures I'd seen paled in comparison to what I was looking at now. The main part of the house rose three stories with a bell tower at its center that thrust up another two. The colors were so intense—those golden stones, the reddish-orange tiles on the roof against a bright blue sky. My gaze swept along the arches and stone pillars that framed the courtyard, then rose to the lacy ironwork that fanned each one of the windows on the second and third floors. Flowers bloomed everywhere, crowding the paths bordering the walks, and spilling out of terra-cotta urns.

Beatrice McKenzie Caulfield, the sister of James McKenzie, the aging patriarch, was responsible for the flowers. I ran through the information I knew about her. She was renowned for her gardening skills and was a frequent participant and speaker at garden shows. In addition to that, she'd run the Hacienda Montega for the past twenty-five years since the untimely death of Elizabeth McKenzie. Beatrice was also the mother of Austin

Caulfield, Cameron's cousin, who'd taken over her job in her absence.

Cole pulled to a stop in front of the courtyard. Inside, I could see a fountain shooting sparks of light back at the sun.

"It's beautiful," I said.

"That it is," Cole agreed. "Does it trigger any memory?"

I glanced at him in surprise.

"Get used to the question, Brooke. The moment you step out of the car, you're Cameron McKenzie, suffering from amnesia. Are you ready?"

I drew in a deep breath and pushed open the door on my side of the car. "Ready."

My step didn't falter once as we walked up the path past the fountain to the huge wood door of the house. Cole knocked. I counted to ten, and Cole had raised his hand to knock again when the door swung open to reveal a small, brown-skinned woman who was as wide as she was tall. She stared at me for a moment, but even as she tucked the towel she was holding into an apron pocket, her face brightened into a smile that was almost as wide as her girth. "Ms. Cameron, Ms. Cameron, you're safe!" She grabbed my hands, drew me over the threshold and enveloped me in a warm hug.

For a moment, she held me tight and I caught the scent of vanilla. Then she drew back, studied me at arm's length, then pulled me in for another hug. "They said you'd be back. Mr. James and Mr. Sloan—they weren't worried. But I…"

When she released me, I saw tears in her eyes. This had to be Elena Santoro, the woman who'd been the housekeeper and cook for the McKenzies for more than forty years. According to Pepper's information, much of the job of raising Cameron had fallen on her shoulders after Elizabeth McKenzie had died.

Elena rubbed the heel of her hand against her cheeks. "I was worried. I shouldn't have." For the first time, she seemed to notice Cole at my side.

"Ma'am." He nodded at her and withdrew his license from his pocket. "I'm Cole Buchanan of Rossi Investigations. Ms. McKenzie here was mugged in San Francisco a little over a month ago, all her ID was stolen, and she's been suffering from amnesia ever since. If the rest of the family is home, perhaps you could let them know we're here, and I could explain everything all at once?"

"You were mugged?" She reached out a hand, hesitated and then dropped it. "You've lost your memory?"

"Yes. Hopefully, it's only temporary. But when I woke up in the hospital, I couldn't remember anything—who I was, where I should go…." Seeing the concern in her eyes, I felt a little twinge of guilt, but it didn't seem to be interfering with my ability to lie. "I hired Mr. Buchanan's security firm to help me find out who I was, and they finally did."

"How awful." She did take my hands then and squeezed them briefly.

"The family?" Cole prompted.

"Yes. But only Ms. Beatrice is here. Mr. Sloan went to Kentucky to pick up a horse and Mr. James is in Los Angeles, having his yearly checkup. Mr. James will be back later today, but Mr. Sloan isn't expected back until tomorrow. Mr. Austin is in Saratoga Springs with Ms. Linton at the races. But Ms. Beatrice is in her office. I'll get her."

Elena bustled away down the hall. For the first time I had time to glance around the huge foyer. The hacienda's interior was no less impressive than its exterior. The floor was covered with honey-colored tiles that offered a nice contrast to the gleaming dark wood of a staircase that swept up to a landing, then split off in two directions to the balconied second level. In the center of the foyer stood a round carved oak table, nearly the size of the one I imagined Arthur had gathered his knights around. On top of it stood a huge crystal vase filled with flowers.

Elena led Beatrice McKenzie Caulfield around the side of the table. My first impression was that Beatrice would have made a great snow queen. Her hair was nearly white, and fell straight and long from a center part almost to her waist. Her eyes were a pale shade of blue, her skin porcelain. Even her clothes were pale. She wore light tan work pants and a shirt in a soft material that seemed to flow as she walked toward us. Her white canvas shoes made no noise as she approached. She was a tall woman, slender, with an ethereal kind of beauty that reminded me of Tennessee Williams's Southern women. Blanche Dubois—but stronger. Colder. I had a feeling that Beatrice would hold her own very well against Stanley Kowalski.

I also had the distinct impression that Beatrice Caulfield had been studying me just as thoroughly as I'd been studying her. When she stopped in front of me, she was the one who broke the silence. "Cameron?"

The word with its question mark came out in a soft voice that somehow matched the rest of her.

"Ma'am," Cole began to tell my story about the accident and my memory loss.

Beatrice interrupted. "Why were you in San Francisco?"

"I don't remember," I said. It was amazing how memory loss came in handy. "Do you have any idea why I might have gone up there?"

She shook her head. "I'm sorry."

Cole continued, telling the part where I came to Rossi Investigations and hired them to find out who I was. He'd nearly finished when a large black cat appeared around the side of the oak table, walked toward us and halted at Elena's feet.

"Hannibal, aren't you happy to see your mistress?" Elena asked.

The cat stayed right where he was, and the look he gave me was not friendly. Did that mean he knew on some cat instinct level that I wasn't Cameron? Here was a complication that I hadn't counted on. Pepper and Cole had warned me there'd be more than one.

Elena scooped Hannibal up and held him out to me.

The cat responded by hissing loudly and taking a swipe at me with his paw.

"Evidently, he's forgotten you already," Beatrice remarked.

"Don't you pay any attention to him, Ms. Cameron," Elena hurried to say. "The two of you were thick as thieves. He just needs some time to get used to you again." She set Hannibal down, and he shot off like a bullet.

I wished that it was as easy to read Beatrice as it was to read the cat. The woman had registered very little emotion at seeing me, but she hadn't shifted her gaze from me once during the time that Cole had talked. I found it impossible to tell from her eyes, but I had a feeling that she didn't harbor any warm feelings for Cameron. Definitely a snow queen, I thought.

Finally, Beatrice turned to Cole. "Would you like something to drink, Mr. Buchanan? Iced tea?"

Cole smiled. "That would be great."

Beatrice had Elena serve us tea on a patio off the kitchen that offered a view of the gardens and the stables in the distance. She was a good hostess and a good listener. By the time we were finished with our drinks, Beatrice knew pretty much everything that had happened to me in the weeks I'd supposedly been missing—everything we wanted her to know.

Finally, she rose. "James will be home late this afternoon. He knew that you'd be back, but I'm sure it will ease his mind to find out that he was right." Then she turned to Cole. "Mr. Buchanan, if you'll leave a card? My brother may wish to speak with you."

Cole took a card out of his pocket and handed it to her.

She turned to me. "Make yourself at home, Cameron. I have work to do in the greenhouse."

I waited until she left before I said to Cole, "Do you think she bought it?"

"I think the jury's out. One of the things that we talked about is that while people may believe you're Cameron, they may suspect you're faking the memory loss. Do you want me to hang around until James gets here?"

"No." I drew in a deep breath and let it out. "I feel like I've been given a little reprieve, not having to explain everything to James and Sloan right away." I was really a bit apprehensive about Sloan and happy that I wouldn't have to face him until the next day. In spite of that I managed a smile for Cole. "I'm going to do a bit of exploring and try to get to know my sister a bit better. I'll be fine. Really."

I walked Cole out to the door and waited until he brought my duffel from the car. In spite of my words, my stomach did a little flip as he pulled away. But in addition to apprehension, I also felt a little thrill of excitement. The adventure was about to begin.

3

A HALF HOUR LATER, I was restlessly exploring
Cameron's bedroom. Elena had taken me up right after
Cole had left, and before I could shut the door, Hannibal
had dashed in, leaped onto the bed and enthroned
himself on the pillows as if he were staking out a claim.

Before I'd let Elena return to the kitchen, I'd asked
her one of the questions that Cole and Pepper and I had
decided we needed to know—a question no one had
bothered with because Cameron had never been
reported missing. Where was each of the cast of characters on the day that Cameron had disappeared? Once
I had the information, I was to phone Pepper and then
Rossi Investigations could check out the alibis. Since
Elena had been able to give such an accurate rundown
of everyone's whereabouts when Cole and I had arrived,
I'd figured she'd be a good source. And she had been.
James and Sloan had been at the ranch that day. Miss
Beatrice had been giving a speech at a flower show in
San Diego about an hour's drive away. Mr. Austin had
been with the Lintons in Las Vegas. There'd been no
censure in her tone, but I sensed that Elena didn't
entirely approve of Austin's whereabouts.

Thanks to Cole's and Pepper's coaching, I knew who

the Lintons were. Marcie Linton was my personal assistant. I'd hired her on about six months ago. Shortly after they'd met, she and Austin had started dating, and they'd since become engaged. Marcie had introduced Austin to her brother, Hal, and the trio had been very close ever since.

Cole had also learned that Hal represented a group of developers who wanted badly to get their hands on a strip of McKenzie land that ran along the Pacific. So far, James had rejected all offers. Evidently, McKenzies didn't part easily with their land.

Once Elena had left, I'd ignored Hannibal, and embarked on the first step in my plan—learning more about my sister. Her bedroom was large and airy with two large floor-to-ceiling windows that opened onto small balconies. In decor the room was feminine—Cameron favored pastels—but it wasn't frilly. The walls were ivory; the rug was an Oriental in muted shades of rose which were picked up in the bedspread and in the upholstered furniture.

In a small alcove, there was a couch—not a love seat, but a full-length couch, one I could imagine stretching out on and reading—or perhaps taking a nap. I tested it, and to my surprise, Hannibal jumped off the bed, ambled over and aimed a glare at me.

In spite of Elena's assurances that cats had short memories and he just needed a little time to get to know his owner again, I couldn't help thinking that Hannibal knew more than he was letting on. "Okay," I said. "Maybe you can sense I'm not Cameron. But I'm trying to find out what happened to her. So we're really on the same side here."

He didn't look convinced.

I didn't have much experience with cats, but I'd handled horses who'd been initially skeptical of my abilities as a rider. The key was never to let them sense your weakness.

I turned to examine the bookcase next to the couch. There, I discovered a variety of books from Shakespeare's Sonnets and well-thumbed copies of classics like *Pride and Prejudice* and *To Kill a Mockingbird* to a thriller about a diamond heist that had recently made the bestseller lists. I'd just read it myself, and I wondered in how many other things my sister's taste and mine might coincide.

From the Queen Anne desk and a delicately hand-carved chair, I assumed she liked antiques. I'd never had the time to hunt for them, but I could appreciate their beauty. On the other side of the couch, I discovered a silly-looking red fox perched on top of an embroidered footstool.

When I picked it up to take a closer look, Hannibal made a growling sound deep in his throat.

I was intimidated enough to put the fox back on the stool, and I turned my attention to the small cabinet. Inside I found a bottle of brandy, a cache of chocolate and a bag of cat tidbits. Had I uncovered the secret to how Cameron and Hannibal had become "thick as thieves?" Selecting one of them, I turned back to the cat.

"Is this what you're hounding me for?"

He moved closer and I gave him the treat. He hadn't been on my list of the players at the hacienda, but if Cameron had kept treats for him right beside her chocolate...

"Look. I'm going to be here for a while, so you'd better get used to me. And I'm not going to steal anything from your mistress. She's my sister."

Hannibal blinked just as if he'd understood what I'd just said.

"We're not enemies. Really. I'm beginning to like her. She has good taste—even in chocolate."

Her cache was made in Switzerland.

Hannibal had no comment. I opened the cabinet, and this time I took out a treat for both of us. As he ate his, I took a bite of chocolate and turned my attention back to the room. Truth told, I not only liked Cameron's taste, I envied it. Since moving to Los Angeles, I'd pretty much buried myself in work, and I hadn't yet taken the time to make my apartment my own.

I investigated Cameron's closet next while Hannibal stood in the doorway to keep watch. What I found was that any possible similarities between my sister and me came to an end when it came to clothes. First off, her closet wasn't a closet. It was a whole room that opened off the larger bed-sitting-room area. My bedroom in my apartment wasn't any larger. One wall housed drawers, cupboards, shoe racks and shelves. Along the other hung Cameron's clothes, neatly arranged and sorted into pants, shirts, jackets, suits and dresses.

If you are what you wear, Cameron McKenzie was a fashion queen. I like clothes, too, but I bought mine off the racks, and Cameron's all came from designer show-rooms. No bargains from Wal-Mart here. So far Jimmy Choo shoes were something that I'd only seen on TV shows. My twin owned four pairs. Way to go, Cameron.

Insatiably curious, I'd searched through drawers and

found she had a taste for gold, expensive lingerie and short nightgowns. I'd even tested her scent—something exotic and French that probably cost more than what I spent on a month's rent.

But it was the bathroom that gave me the biggest surprise about my sister. The best description I could come up with was that it was like a little slice of paradise. There was a skylight situated so that sun, rain or starlight would be visible from the tub. There were gleaming marble tiles, a shower with frosted glass doors, brass faucets, and enough plants hanging and bursting out of pots to make one think of Eden.

I was aware of all that as I stood in the doorway, but my eyes never left the tub. Surrounding it on a wide ledge were glass bottles in various hues, filled no doubt with scents and oils and creams. And I counted twelve candles. The tub itself sank into the floor and it was big enough for two. I couldn't help wondering if it had ever been used that way. Cameron and Sloan? My sister definitely had a sensuous side.

That shouldn't surprise me. So did I. At least I was pretty sure I did. I just hadn't had much time to indulge it—or perhaps, I hadn't had much of a reason to indulge it. Cameron had her very attractive fiancé.

Turning, I moved back into the bedroom and began to pace. Bottom line, after an hour in my sister's bedroom, I'd learned she had excellent taste in decor, expensive taste in clothes and the money to indulge it, and a passionate side to her nature—all of which I admired and envied her for.

To top it off, she was going to be heir to half of her father's kingdom—worth millions of dollars.

Compared to hers, my life seemed rather mundane.

But my purpose here wasn't about me, I reminded myself. I was here to learn all I could about Cameron and just why she might have disappeared on that day five weeks ago.

Moving to the window, I focused on what my next move should be. I'd fully expected to spend my first day on the ranch meeting all the major players that I would have to convince that I was Cameron without a memory. With Sloan and James away, I was out of plot line. The view from Cameron's bedroom was the same as the one Beatrice, Cole and I had had on the patio, and my eyes were drawn to the stables. If Sloan had been here, I would have asked him for a tour and perhaps gone for a ride. It had been so long since I'd been on a horse.

But that might not be my best move. I was suffering from memory loss. So it might look strange if I walked down to the stables and asked someone to saddle up a horse. My gaze moved to the hills that bordered the valley the ranch sat in on the east and the west.

But I could ask for a car. After all, I was Cameron McKenzie, home after an absence of five weeks. Memory loss or not, I might be interested in driving around to see if something, anything stirred a memory.

It certainly beat sitting here in Cameron's room with a cat who seemed to value me only for my ability to provide food. Elena would know whom I'd have to speak to. I hurried to the door, opened it, and then glanced back at Hannibal. He was back on the bed, sitting on his throne. "Coming?"

He made no move.

"See you later," I said as I let myself out and shut the door.

ELENA HAD GIVEN ME the keys to an SUV that was parked right outside the kitchen. It had a McKenzie Ranch logo on the side, and anybody who needed to run an errand could use it. On impulse and out of curiosity, I'd driven up onto the bluff that formed a natural boundary on one side of the valley the ranch lay snuggled in. The road was unpaved and rough in spots. When I'd gone as far as I could with the SUV, I'd parked it and walked another half mile along a path that wove in and out of boulders until I'd reached the top.

All around me as far as I could see, lay the vast stretch of land that the McKenzies could lay claim to. I knew from the maps that Cole and Pepper had shown me that the shores of the Pacific were blocked by more hills behind me, but the estate extended all the way to the sea. Below me the ground sloped gently before it dropped off sharply into the valley below. Since I have a problem with heights, I was careful not to go near the edge. My view of the hacienda itself was still blocked by some of the boulders that dotted the bluff, so I walked farther along the narrow path to get a better look.

The wind had picked up, and to the west I could see huge dark clouds racing in from the Pacific. Thunder growled in the distance, and lightning split the sky.

Shades of Wuthering Heights, I thought. Not a good omen. Then I resolutely turned my back on the approaching storm and walked onward until I had a good view of the flat stretch of land in the little valley below.

From this vantage point, I could see everything that I hadn't been able to see from the patio or Cameron's window. Behind the hacienda there was an Olympic-sized pool and a pool house surrounded by trees and terraced gardens. Fanning off from that I could see orange groves, tennis courts and what must be Beatrice's greenhouses.

If Beatrice was responsible for all of that, my hat was off to her. The stables, along with the training and riding rings and what was probably once the original carriage house, were a short distance away. Here and there, I caught glimpses of a stream twisting like a silver snake in and out among trees which grew thicker in some places than in others.

And this was only the ranch land. The entire McKenzie estate, I reminded myself, included that prime undeveloped real estate along the Pacific Coast. All I could think was *Wow!*

Far below me, a truck pulling a horse trailer drew up in front of the largest of the stable buildings. A second later, two men climbed out and the larger of the two, the driver, went immediately to open the trailer door. Even at this distance, I could tell that the horse he led out by a tether was magnificent. Huge and black, the animal reared up as if he just had to stretch after being cooped up. I grinned, thinking that I'd felt the same way myself just a short time ago.

Then, instead of leading the horse into the stables, I watched the man leap up onto the horse's back and ride him bareback across the nearest field. Admiration and envy streamed through me as rider and horse took the first fence and began to make their way toward the very hills I was perched on.

I let my gaze sweep the estate again as I struggled to identify the other emotions tumbling through me. Excitement and pride that all of this belonged to my twin sister. Reading Pepper's report and studying the photos had whetted my curiosity. Now, seeing the hacienda, the land, from this vantage point was making Cameron even more real to me. But I wanted to know more. I needed to know everything. Obviously, we shared a love of horses, and hers had been easily nurtured here.

Although it had always been a dream of mine, I'd yet to own a horse of my own. My parents had pointed out the difficulties involved with trying to stable and care for one in Chicago. Aside from the expense, would it be fair to the horse? They'd been right, of course. They usually were. And they hadn't stood in the way of riding lessons. Although they hadn't been enthused when I'd wanted to try steeplechasing, they'd come to see me do it. In college I'd been a member of the riding club.

I'd often thought that it must have been hard for them to have a daughter who was so different from them. Oh, they loved me. But there'd always been that sort of bemused expression on their faces when I'd excelled in a field that was so outside of their own areas of interest. They were left brained, and I was right. I found myself wondering if they'd ever regretted not having a child of their own. I also wondered if Cameron had fit in better with her adopted family.

Thunder cracked and lightning split the sky, but I ignored both. Instead, I continued to think about my twin. Would a love of horses, of riding, be genetic?

Wardrobes aside, in what other ways was I like Cameron—or not like her? Would she be able to understand me in a way my parents never had? More than ever, I felt the need to find out.

And soon. The more I saw of the ranch and the kind of life that Cameron had, the more I wondered why she would disappear.

Thunder boomed overhead this time, and the lightning flashed to my left almost simultaneously. I thought I smelled it. Below me, a line of pitch-black shadows raced across the valley reminding me of a shade being drawn down for the night. In the murkier light, the hacienda made me think of Thornfield, Manderley, the Château de Valmy and every other mysterious mansion gracing the pages of those Gothic novels I'd read as a girl. I thought again of the fact that the mistresses of this mansion had seemed to succumb to untimely ends, and a chill skittered its way up my spine.

Ridiculous, I told myself. If I was ever going to pull this impersonation off, I would have to keep a tight rein on my imagination. This was a working horse ranch, not some Gothic mansion plagued by secrets and long-covered-up murders.

On the other hand, my twin sister who stood to inherit at least half of all of this was missing. People had been killed for much less than this. Another chill moved through me.

Then the sky opened, and rain poured down so thick and fast that I could barely make out the path as I turned and began to wind my way back to the car.

The good news was I was still wearing the jeans, plain T-shirt and sneakers that I'd worn for my ride out to the McKenzie estate. The bad news was that I was soaked to the bone by the time I'd taken three steps and my new "Cameron" hairdo was destroyed. Pushing the sodden mess out of my eyes, I stretched my hands out in front of me like a sleepwalker. The car was too far away to seek shelter there, so I stumbled toward the darker shape of what had to be one of the boulders I'd skirted earlier. Once I reached it, I moved around to the far side and let it block the wind and at least some of the rain. Then I hunkered down to wait out the storm.

I wasn't sure how long I squatted at the side of the boulder—probably not longer than five or ten minutes. The storm ended as quickly as it had begun. The rain stopped first, and gradually the sun began to peek through clouds that were quickly blowing away. As I rose to my feet, I could still hear thunder grumbling in the distance. I'd made my way around the boulder and back onto the path before it finally registered in my mind that the rhythmic pounding I was listening to wasn't just thunder. It was also hoofbeats.

Realization came at the same instant that horse and rider shot around a curve in the path less than fifty yards from where I was standing. My heart lodged in my throat, my body froze, and my imagination took flight. Burned into my mind was the image of horse and man, all muscle and speed, moving in perfect unity—the mythic centaur in the flesh. In that instant, I wasn't sure which animal was more magnificent—man or beast.

Luckily, the man had quick reflexes. He reined the horse in sharply. The animal reared, protesting loudly. It might have been the sound of the horse's distress or perhaps it was the sight of those powerful hooves that jolted me free of the trance I'd been in, but I finally leaped toward the side of the path. I landed hard on the uneven ground, felt my ankle twist and give out just before I crashed into the boulder.

Behind me I heard the struggle between horse and rider, the horse neighing, a deep male voice talking in a soothing tone. Turning, I saw the horse rear again, but the man's hands remained steady on the rope, and he continued to talk in a firm tone.

"Easy, Saturn. Easy, boy."

I suddenly realized that this must be the same man I'd seen take the horse out of the trailer and ride him bareback across the fields. Not only had he kept control of the stallion and saved me from injury, he'd also remained seated. Admiration streamed through me. I had some idea of the skill it was taking to calm the frightened horse.

I was sitting in the shade of the boulder, but the horse and the man were bathed now in sunlight and I was able to take in more details. The man had slid from the horse and stood with his back toward me, talking to the horse and keeping a firm grip on the tether. He and the animal had a lot in common. Both were large and dark and strong—perfectly matched in the struggle that was going on. The man's hair curled around the nape of his neck. He was broad in the shoulders, lean in the hips, and long in the legs. With his jeans and chambray shirt plastered to him like a second skin, I could see the movement of each sculpted muscle as he quieted the horse with patient skill. The horse, still frightened, reared again and pawed the air. The stallion was larger, stronger. But the battle wouldn't be decided on size alone. It would come down to who had the stronger will.

The man let out the rope, then drew it in again, each time getting closer to the horse. The closer he drew, the calmer the horse became. It was like watching a slow, steady dance of seduction. Admiration and something else I was much less familiar with moved through me and settled in a hot little pool in my center. I had the strangest sensation that I was melting. Then his hands were on the horse, moving gently and firmly over those muscles, while he continued to talk, to croon almost. I had no idea how long I sat there in the shadow of the boulder watching man and horse.

And imagining what it would feel like to have those hands on me.

"Are you all right?" His focus was still on the horse, and since he asked the question in the same tone he'd been using to quiet the animal, it took me a moment to realize that he was speaking to me.

"Yes." My voice was so breathless I didn't recognize it. "I'm fine." To prove it, I dug my fingers into a crevice in the boulder and pulled myself to my feet. I'd totally forgotten about my ankle, and when I put my full weight on it, I sat right back down with a little squeal.

He turned toward me then. "You're hurt. Did one of his hooves…" His voice trailed off and his eyes narrowed. "Cameron? I didn't recognize you at first."

Of course he hadn't. I could understand that. I hadn't recognized him, either. He'd been intent on calming the horse, and I'd been equally intent on him. It was only now as he quickly tethered the horse and strode toward me that I realized this was Sloan Campbell, my sister Cameron's fiancé.

"You could have been killed."

The anger in his voice was clear—even though it was tightly leashed. And the simple truth of his statement had a chill moving up my spine. He was no less intimidating than when he'd been thundering toward me on the top of the horse. There he'd looked mythical. Now he looked tough, arrogant and furious. He'd evidently spent all of his patience on Saturn.

Why had it taken me so long to realize who he was? I'd certainly spent enough time studying his photos. Perhaps it was because the magnetism I'd sensed in the pictures was even more potent in real life.

"How badly are you hurt?" His tone was sharp with accusation.

"I'm not hurt. The horse didn't touch me. I just twisted my ankle. I—"

He dropped to his knees and focused his attention on my ankle.

"It's swollen," he said. His fingers were as gentle as they'd been on the horse as they moved the wet jeans up my legs. While he probed my ankle, I found myself staring at his hands—the long fingers, the wide palms—and I tried to ignore the warmth that was unfurling in little ribbons up my leg. Other men had touched me, some casually, others intimately, but I'd never felt this kind of intensity before.

Adrenaline. I'd nearly been run down by the horse. That's why I was reacting this way.

"I don't think it's broken." I heard relief in his tone. "Are you hurt anywhere else?" He glanced up at me then.

"No. You handled the horse beautifully. I'm—" Every other word I intended to say slipped out of my mind as I met his penetrating gaze. His eyes...they were dark gray, the color of the kind of fog that could swallow you up and make you lose all sense of direction. I suddenly felt as though I were losing mine.

Then as if he'd satisfied himself that I was all right, he grabbed my shoulders and gave me a quick shake. "Where the hell have you been for the past five weeks?"

SLOAN TOOK A DEEP BREATH and clamped down hard on the all-too-familiar emotions swirling through him. Anger, annoyance, relief. Those were the standard feelings that Cameron had been able to pull out of him ever since they'd been kids and his job had frequently been to get her out of scrapes.

But not this time. Five weeks ago when she'd first run off, he'd understood her need to get away and think. The truth was, he'd needed some time himself. But as the weeks had rolled by, understanding had turned into annoyance and finally into anger.

"Five weeks is a long time. Couldn't you have at least called your father to let him know you were safe?"

"I couldn't. I—"

"Couldn't? Or maybe you expected me to come running after you and drag you back here so that you could save face?"

"Save face?"

He barely kept himself from shaking her again. In spite of the fact that James McKenzie had claimed he was confident that Cameron would return when she'd had time to think everything through, the old man had been worried. Hell, he'd begun to worry himself—and now she'd returned, looking so damned innocent. It had been years since Cameron had tried to use that innocent look on him.

That realization was what had him narrowing his eyes and studying her more carefully. There was something about her...something he couldn't quite put his finger on. Her eyes were that same brilliant shade of green, but they seemed different. Darker. And there was something in them right now. Something that he'd never seen before. Arousal?

The sudden response in his gut was also new. He tightened his grip on her arms. "What the hell kind of game are you playing?"

4

HE THOUGHT I was playing a game? I struggled to get my mind around what he'd just said. But as long as I was looking into Sloan Campbell's eyes, my brain felt numb. My body, on the other hand, was far from numb. My senses were operating at full power. Sloan was only touching my shoulders, yet I could feel the pressure of each one of his fingers—hot like a brand on my skin. He was so close that I could catch the scent of rain and horse, so close that I could feel his breath on my lips. So close that if I leaned forward just a bit, I could taste him.

Don't move, I told myself. Don't move. But I was shocked at how hard it was not to.

"Well?" He prodded me with another little shake, and it helped.

"I'm sorry." My voice and my mouth were finally working. Now it was up to my brain. And he was right. I was playing a game, so I'd better make my first move. "I don't remember being Cameron. I am. I must be, but I just don't remember."

"Come again." He dropped his hands then, but I could feel those eyes boring into me while I told him my story—the mugging, the fact that my purse had never been recovered so there'd been no way for the police to identify me. When I told him about waking up in the hospital and not having any idea who I was, I had the distinct impression that he could see right into me, that he knew what I was thinking. A little tendril of fear worked its way up my spine. Sloan Campbell might have a gentle side, but I sensed that this was a man who could be hard when he wanted to be.

"You're saying that you don't remember anything before you were mugged?"

His tone was skeptical, but I'd expected that. I could handle it. After all, how many people encountered a person who'd lost their memory in real life? Mostly, it occurred as a plot device in movies, romance novels, or soap operas. "My doctor assures me it's temporary."

"If you don't remember who you are, how did you get here?"

That explanation I had down pat. I told him how I'd hired Rossi Investigations to find out who I was. "It took them a while because no one ever filed a missing persons report."

"We assumed you'd come back after you'd sorted things out." His tone was neutral. I couldn't tell if he was buying the memory loss or not. I wasn't an actress. I just wrote story lines for professionals who could bring them to life.

Then he was quiet for so long that nerves knotted in my stomach. To fill the void, I said, "I drove one of the SUV's up here to see if getting a bird's-eye view of the ranch would stir up some memories."

"Did it?"

"No."

"Do I look familiar to you?"

I shook my head. "I don't remember you, but I recognize you from the newspaper clippings the P.I.'s gave me. You're Sloan Campbell, Cameron's—my fiancé."

Tilting his head to one side, he continued to study me. "I'm not sure what kind of game you're playing."

The man's eyes were mesmerizing, and for a moment, just one mad moment, I was tempted to confess. Then I thought of Cameron and what I'd come here to do. "That's the second time you've said that. Why are you so sure I'm playing a game?"

He touched me then, just the brush of a finger along my jawline. "Because you're all about games. And you're a sore loser."

"Loser?" I had no idea what he meant. I was finding it very hard to think while he was touching me.

Without warning, Sloan slid his hand to the back of my neck and touched his mouth to mine. I didn't move. I couldn't. The kiss was so soft. He didn't press, didn't demand. He simply tasted very gently. Still a riot of sensations moved through me.

Don't respond, I told myself. But I could feel my lips soften and part. I could feel my whole body melt.

All the time he watched me with those gray, knowing eyes. I had to clench my fingers into my palms to keep from grabbing him. I wanted to use my hands on him, to drag them through his hair, to test the muscles under that shirt. All the while his taste poured into me until I was nearly drunk with it. With him.

When he drew back, I took a minute and prayed that my voice would be steady. Then I said, "What was that for?"

He regarded me for a moment through narrowed eyes. "A welcome back."

But I knew it had been a test. What I wasn't sure of was whether or not I'd passed.

"C'mon." His tone turned brisk as he took my arm and helped me to my feet. "Let's see if you can walk on that ankle."

I concentrated on doing that. This time I was careful when I put weight on it, but it held. "It'll probably be weak for a few days."

Without comment, he led me over to where Saturn was still munching grass. Then he cupped his hands. "I'll give you a leg up."

I didn't pretend to misunderstand. He intended for me to ride the horse. "I drove up here in an SUV."

"It's your right ankle you twisted. It would probably be better if you didn't drive until it's stronger. I'll send someone up to fetch your car."

Still I hesitated. I had a feeling that as far as Sloan was concerned, this was another test. I just wasn't quite sure what to do to pass it.

"Once he lets off a little steam, Saturn can be a perfect gentleman. If I'd put him in his stall right after taking him out of the trailer, he might have kicked a hole in one of the stable walls. But he'll be fine now."

Turning toward the horse, I raised a hand and ran it down his neck. "Hate to be confined, do you? I can sympathize with that."

To my surprise and delight, Saturn neighed softly and turned his head to nuzzle my shoulder. I laughed as I looked at Sloan. "He's quite a flirt."

Sloan didn't return my smile. Instead, he just

regarded me with an odd expression in his eyes. "You don't usually flirt back."

I had a feeling that I'd failed some sort of test, so I figured I might as well go for broke. Placing my good foot in his cupped hands, I grabbed a handful of Saturn's mane and swung myself up onto his back.

When I looked down at Sloan, he was still studying me. "He likes you, Red."

"Red? Is that what you call me?"

A mocking glint came into Sloan's eyes. "You tell me when you get your memory back."

I met his eyes steadily. I was going to have to learn to hold my own with this man. "You still think I'm playing some kind of game, don't you?"

Without answering, he swung himself up behind me, then reached around me to gather both ends of the rope into his hands. "The jury's out on that one. I'll let you know when I decide. In the meantime, you'll have to tell your story to your father." He raised a hand and pointed to the road that wound its way from the main highway to the ranch. "I believe that's his car right now. If we hurry, we'll reach the ranch about the same time he does."

Sloan urged Saturn down the slope. Then he added, "James McKenzie is not an easy man to fool."

SLOAN CAMPBELL WASN'T an easy man to fool, either. He loosened the tension on the rope to give Saturn more freedom to make his way down the slope. He was a man who prided himself on his ability to size up people as well as horseflesh. But "Red"—he'd decided to call her that until he figured out who she was—Red had had him going there for a few moments.

He had to admit that she was a dead ringer for Cameron, but his gut instinct told him that whoever she was, she wasn't Cameron McKenzie. He let his gaze drift to the distinctive red hair, and wondered if hers had come out of a bottle. She had the same slender build, the same surprisingly long legs, considering the fact that she was barely five foot four. In body type and coloring, she could have been Cameron's twin.

Except Cameron didn't have a twin.

Still, whatever annoyance he felt for being taken in by "Red," however temporarily, was more than matched by the admiration he felt for her guts and her creativity. He'd come damned close to buying her memory loss story. He might have if it weren't for her eyes.

He'd seen something when he'd first grabbed her that he'd never seen in Cameron's eyes. Desire. It wasn't something a man could miss, and it had triggered a response in him. The kiss had been a test, and he wasn't pleased by the fact that he'd wanted for a moment to take it beyond a test. What he'd felt when his mouth had pressed against hers had been raw and stunning. And for one brief moment, with her taste pouring into him, he'd wanted to go further. The only reason he hadn't was because he hadn't been sure he could stop himself from taking her right there on the bluff.

No woman had ever pushed him that far that quickly before. Certainly not Cameron. The kiss had been the clincher. The slender woman sitting in front of him was not Cameron McKenzie. But that left the questions— who the hell was she? And where was Cameron?

When Saturn finally reached level ground, Sloan urged him into a trot. His annoyance with himself deepened at the fact that he'd never once questioned that Cameron had run away in a snit five weeks ago. James hadn't questioned it, either. No one had. She hadn't taken her car, but she often used a limo service, claiming that being driven allowed her to get work done.

The night before she'd left, he and Cameron had had words, and she'd threatened to back out of the wedding, and he'd told her to go ahead. Not that he thought she would. Though six years separated them, they'd grown up together, and he knew her very well. She was high-strung, used to getting her own way, and he'd figured she'd stayed away five weeks to figure out a way to come back, go through with the wedding and still save face.

She wasn't going to back out of the wedding. She'd given her word to her father. And while she might be spoiled, Cameron McKenzie never went back on her word. He'd convinced himself that she'd stayed away out of pride.

He'd told "Red" nothing less than the truth. Cameron liked to play games, and she didn't like to lose. Had she found a double and set up this little charade by herself? For what purpose? But if she hadn't set it up, he didn't like the alternative explanations.

His gaze shifted again to the woman sitting in front of him, and his glance fell on the delicate curve of her neck right where it joined her shoulder. Arousal bloomed inside of him again, as raw and primitive as it had been when he'd kissed her.

The attraction he felt for her was going to be a problem. And he'd have to handle it.

Because the alternative was that Red was up to her neck in Cameron's disappearance. A missing heiress and a ringer who was trying to take her place just a month before the wedding? He didn't like that scenario one bit.

And Red might not be in this alone. There were groups of developers who would do a lot to get their hands on that strip of land along the Pacific. Sloan frowned. He liked that scenario even less.

He just had to figure out which way to play it. To play her. He wouldn't let James or anyone else know his suspicions. No need to worry the old man before he had some evidence or at least a clearer idea of what had happened to Cameron. Besides, he might learn something from letting Red play out her little charade. Give her enough rope and she just might hang herself.

One thing was certain. Until he knew exactly what her game was, he was going to keep her on a very short leash.

SLOAN SAID NOTHING MORE on the ride back to the ranch, but I was intensely aware of him behind me on the horse. When we arrived, we rode past the stables and up a path that led to the back of the house. He dismounted, but before I could follow suit, hard hands gripped my waist and the next second I was on the ground. "Be careful when you put weight on that ankle."

He didn't step back right away. He just looked at me as if there was some answer in my eyes that he was determined to extract. If I'd known what it was, I would have given it to him.

By the time he dropped his hands, my knees had gone weak so I was very careful as I followed his advice and tested my ankle gingerly. "It's fine."

"I'm going to leave you in the kitchen with Elena.

She'll have an Ace bandage, and you'd better ice it tonight."

I looked at him then, but his expression was unreadable. I wished that I could figure him out. Then maybe I could control my reaction to him. One minute, I was sure he was mocking me or testing me. The next he was kind and thinking of something like an Ace bandage.

Or kissing me. I was trying very hard not to think of that kiss.

An ancient-looking man, who had the slight build of a jockey, and the wrinkled face of Rumplestiltskin had followed us up the path and now took the rope from Sloan.

"Make sure you walk him in one of the rings and cool him down, Gus."

The old man snorted. "You're telling me how to handle a horse? I was working them before you were born."

Sloan laughed as he turned to me. "Ms. Cameron's back, but she doesn't recognize you because she's lost her memory."

Gus shifted his gaze to me and nodded. "Welcome back, Ms. Cameron." His eyes were nearly as penetrating as Sloan's, but I saw a twinkle in them. "Lace Ribbons will be happy to see you. I've seen that she's been exercised regularly while you've been gone." Then with another nod, he turned and led Saturn away.

"He likes me," I said.

The look Sloan gave me was enigmatic. "He's known you since you were able to get down to the stables on your own." Taking my arm, Sloan urged me onto the patio where I'd had tea earlier with Cole and Beatrice and then into the house.

"Now that Gus is spreading the word of your return,

I want to be the first to let James know. I'll help him get settled in his rooms, and then I'll send for you. It might be too much of a shock if you just walk in."

"Fine." I watched him head toward the main foyer. That would give me a reprieve—and a little time out of Sloan Campbell's disturbing presence.

As I made my way to the kitchen, I heard Elena welcoming James—my father. I was going to have to start thinking of him that way, I reminded myself.

In the meantime, I really needed to figure Sloan out. The fact that I was attracted to him—and there was no use denying that anymore—meant that I wasn't thinking clearly about him. But I knew enough from creating characters that most people were defined by their motivations—the whys. What were Sloan's? My instinct told me that he was not buying my story entirely. But *why* wasn't he?

Did he have some reason to know for certain that I was not Cameron suffering from amnesia? I stopped short in the middle of the kitchen as I realized one reason he might have for seeing right through my little masquerade. Was Sloan Campbell responsible for my sister's disappearance?

5

JAMES MCKENZIE'S ROOMS were at the back of the house, Elena informed me as she led the way along a corridor. After helping put an Ace bandage on my ankle, she'd taken me to Cameron's room and waited while I changed my clothes and freshened up a bit.

It was my first opportunity to dress in my sister's clothes. Pressed for time, I'd settled on a pair of navy cotton trousers with a white silk blouse and pulled on the closest pair of boots. Luckily, everything had fit. I had stories all ready in case they hadn't. "I lost weight after the accident." Or, "I gained some weight after the accident."

On impulse, I'd grabbed some of Cameron's scent out of a crystal bottle and dabbed it on. It was more exotic than the kind I usually favored, but I'd thought it might help with the cat. And much to my relief and surprise, it had. When I'd stepped out of the closet room, Hannibal hadn't hissed or attacked. He'd simply sent me a bland look from his little "throne."

"See. He's beginning to remember you," Elena had said.

Privately, I figured that Hannibal's more friendly attitude had more to do with his newfound access to cat treats than with memory.

"This is it," Elena announced as she halted in front of the door at the end of the corridor. At her knock, I heard a voice boom, "C'mon in."

When Elena stepped aside, I drew in a deep breath, then, opening the door, I walked in.

And froze. The room was impressive to say the least. It was large, nearly thirty feet long and a good twenty feet wide. Light poured in through three windows that stretched from floor to ceiling and nearly filled the far wall. Each one had a balcony with a lacy wrought iron balustrade, and each was topped with stained glass.

Sloan stood leaning against one of the window frames, his face in the shadows. But I could feel that he was looking at me. James was seated in a thronelike chair to his right. There was a large ornately carved desk in front of him. Through a door to my left, I glimpsed the foot of a bed. The wall to my right was filled with bookshelves. Leather sofas and chairs were clustered on honey-colored wood floors. There was even a game table with a chess set at the ready.

The whole effect was homey and inviting.

"Come closer, gal. I can't see you while you're standing in the shadows."

The deep voice carried the same authority that I'd noticed earlier in Sloan's, and I moved forward, suddenly and overwhelmingly curious to see the man who'd raised my sister. Pepper had shown me a photo, but as I drew closer, I saw that it hadn't done him justice.

James McKenzie was as impressive as the room. He was a large bear of a man, and in spite of the fact that arthritis had largely confined him to his wheelchair, his complexion was still ruddy, and he was strikingly handsome. Though his hair was streaked with white, I could tell that it had been red at one time. But it was his eyes that held my attention. In the short time that I'd been standing there, I knew that I had been quickly and thoroughly summed up. That ability to cut through everything and see right to the core was another thing that he shared with Sloan, I thought.

Did that mean he was going to be just as suspicious of me as Sloan was?

"Surprised that I'm still alive, are ya?"

"No. I mean...I don't..."

"Remember anything," he finished for me. "Sloan filled me in on your mugging. It's the only reason that I'm not giving you a dressing-down for putting us through all this worry."

I glanced at Sloan, but with the light shining through the windows behind him, I still couldn't see his expression.

When I looked back, James was still studying me with an almost hungry look in his eyes. And I thought I saw a trace of sadness, too. Or regret? Wasn't he happy that I was back?

James rose from his chair and extended his arms. "Come give me a hug, gal. I've missed them. And you."

I moved around the desk and walked into James's outstretched arms. "Welcome home. It's good to have you here."

The words and the fierceness of his hug warmed me. My parents had never been much for showing affection in a physical way, and I found myself envying my sister. On impulse, I wrapped my arms around James and held tight for a moment. "I'm really glad to be here." And I was.

When he finally drew back, James studied me for a minute. "You don't remember anything?"

I shook my head. "I'm sorry. I don't even remember how I ended up in San Francisco."

He released me and eased back down in his chair. "You seen anything yet that triggers a memory?"

"No. I went through my room and my clothes, and I rode up into the hills to get a view of the whole ranch, but it was like I'd never seen any of it before."

"Good. Keep at it," James said. "The sooner we get you back to normal the better. I've discussed it with Sloan, and I'm going to contact the rest of the family and summon them here for a dinner party tonight to welcome you home. Your cousin Austin's in Saratoga Springs, but he's got the jet. You up to it?"

"Sure." My stomach lurched a bit, but what else could I say?

Sloan circled the desk so that he stood with me in front of it. "James's theory is that seeing one or more of them may help you remember. I'm more of the opinion that meeting them all en masse might cause you to run away again." The two men exchanged a look that held both understanding and humor.

He loves the old man, I thought. It was then that I realized that Sloan had come here to pave the way for me, not out of kindness to me, but because he truly loved James. My admiration for him moved up a notch.

"Don't let Sloan sour you against your kinfolk," James said with a grin. "We'll let them do that all on their own."

Sloan laughed then, and the rich sound filled the air. I found myself smiling at him, and he smiled back.

There was no mockery in his eyes this time. But I could see something else, something more intimate and it had something hot spreading through me. The heat kicked up several degrees when he lifted a hand and with one finger traced a little half circle under my eye. "You're tired, Red. You'd better rest so that you're up to handling them and dealing with their questions."

I couldn't move. I was sure my legs had turned to water. He'd barely touched me, but I felt it clear down to my toes.

He dropped his hand abruptly and turned to James. "I have to get back to work." Without another word, he strode to the door and opened it.

I stared after him, finally accepting what I had tried to deny before. I was attracted to Sloan Campbell. Big-time. I'd been attracted from the moment I'd first seen his picture, and it had only increased when we'd met face-to-face on the bluff and he'd kissed me. I could no longer blame it on adrenaline. It was lust.

My stomach knotted. I'd come here to learn all I could about my sister, to find a clue to her where-abouts—not to fall in lust with her fiancé. And I couldn't yet dismiss the possibility that he might have had some-thing to do with her disappearance. These were the kind of plot complications that would be great for *Secrets*. But they should not be happening to nothing-ever-happens-to-me Brooke Ashby.

At the door, Sloan turned back and looked at me. I realized something else. He knew exactly what effect he was having on me.

What in the world had I gotten myself into?

"Take a nap," he said in that authoritative way he had.

"You'll be here for dinner," James said to him.

"I wouldn't miss it."

When Sloan closed the door, I turned to face James and there was a moment of awkward silence between us.

"He's a good man," James finally said.

"Yes." So far, I could agree with that assessment.

"He'll make you a good husband."

I didn't have an answer ready for that. But I sensed that Cameron and he had had this conversation before. "Do you have any idea why I ran away?"

James watched for a moment. "Everyone figured it was bridal jitters."

I studied him right back. He was a man who was used to getting what he wanted. "And I'm the type of coward who would have run away?"

"No." I saw a flash of something in his eyes. Pride? "But you're headstrong and you have a temper. You and Sloan had a little argument the day before you disappeared."

"About what?"

James shrugged. "You'll have to ask him."

"So I ran away to punish him?" I could understand that my sister, the woman that I was coming to know, might have done that.

"You ran away to think," James corrected. "From the time you were a little girl, you liked to get away from everything and think."

Something moved through me. I'd always done the same thing. Wasn't that one of the reasons I'd borrowed the SUV and driven up into the hills? "So you weren't surprised when I just disappeared?"

"No. I knew you'd eventually get it all figured out and then you'd come home. And I was right." He smiled at me. "Marriage is a big step. But it's always better when there's love and at least a bit of chemistry involved, right?"

I nodded, not sure where he was going.

"You and Sloan have the chemistry. The love will follow. Now go on and get out of here, gal." He waved his hands at me. "I'm an old man and I need a nap before the festivities begin."

MY THOUGHTS AND EMOTIONS were still spinning as I left James's suite and hurried back to Cameron's room. I'd better keep reminding myself of that—Cameron's room, Cameron's family, Cameron's fiancé.

But when I reached the room, I found Hannibal still reclining on the pillows at the head of the bed. The look he gave me was not friendly. I wasn't in the mood for a turf war, so I went to the cabinet and got us both a treat. It wasn't enough to lure him off the pillows, but he didn't give me any grief when I stretched out well away from him on the foot of the bed and bit into chocolate.

For a while, I closed my eyes and let my thoughts spin in my head. This was a technique I often used when I was working on story lines. Complications were great when I was developing ideas for a plot, but they were trickier to handle in real life.

What I'd learned so far about my sister and her disappearance confirmed what had been in Pepper's report. Cameron was a bit headstrong and spoiled, so no one had been very alarmed when she'd disappeared. James thought her sudden flight might have been triggered by a lover's quarrel. I made a mental note to find out what she and Sloan had quarreled about.

Though he hadn't said it outright, James had hinted that Cameron and Sloan were not in love, but had a chemistry between them. I could relate to that. My reaction to Sloan Campbell was pure chemistry.

But he was my sister's fiancé, her future husband. *Big* complication! If Mallory Carstairs were faced with the problem, I knew exactly what the "bad girl" diva would do. She'd jump his bones.

Hannibal made a growl-like noise from the head of the bed. When I opened my eyes to check on him, he growled again. Could he read my mind?

I made a second trip to the cabinet and got more treats.

"Don't worry," I told him as I tossed one at him. "I'm not Mallory Carstairs." No matter that I'd like to have her guts. My sister had disappeared, and I'd come here, impersonating her, to find out what had happened to her. If my plan was going to have any chance of success, my best strategy would be to steer clear of Sloan Campbell.

Plopping myself once more at the foot of the bed, I let chocolate melt on my tongue. The problem was he might know more than anyone else about what had happened to Cameron. So I was caught between a rock and a hard place. I was going to have to handle Sloan Campbell very carefully—and at the same time keep my hands off of him.

This time, the sound Hannibal made sounded suspiciously like a snort.

6

WHEN I APPROACHED the door of the main parlor that evening, I felt a little like Cinderella arriving late at the ball. She too must have feared that she'd be exposed for the imposter she was when she'd first entered that ballroom.

I'd slept for two hours. I might have been out even longer except that Hannibal had decided to nudge me awake—and off the bed. I couldn't help thinking that he knew I didn't belong in Cameron's bed. I'd bribed him with another treat and that had settled him as I'd raced around dressing for dinner.

I'd chosen the first dress I'd looked at—a simple black sheath that fit as if it had been made for me. I'd recognized the designer label, and realized that my twin had probably spent more on that one outfit than I would spend on clothes for the next year. The strappy sandals I'd settled on would have taken care of my budget for the year after that. But when I stood in front of the mirror and saw myself, I'd definitely envied Cameron. And I had felt different somehow. More like Cameron?

The memory of that feeling gave me the courage to step into the parlor. The room was large, just short of cavernous. In the wall across from me four sets of French doors stood open to showcase a breathtaking view of the gardens. The scent of flowers mingled with burning candles, and there was music, soft strings beneath the clink of glasses and the buzz of conversation.

Paintings were scattered over ivory-colored walls— scenes of the ranch, I decided. The style was simple and compelling, and the artist had captured the beauty of the land. I wondered who had painted them. Suddenly, I became aware that one by one conversations had halted, and everyone had turned to stare at me.

A little bubble of panic moved through me as I scanned the faces. People were clustered in groups down the length of the room, and there were more than I'd anticipated. Definitely more than family.

"Cameron, there you are. Come in. Come in." James's voice boomed down the length of the room. He was seated in a wheelchair tonight but even framed by the huge fireplace that filled one wall of the room, he managed to look larger than life. "Sloan, fix your fiancée a drink."

Sloan appeared at my side, causing me to wonder if he'd stationed himself near the entrance for just that reason. He wore an open-collar shirt and lightweight blazer with jeans and boots.

"What would you like to drink, Red?" he asked as he led me to the drink cart.

"Wine. White," I replied.

"White wine?" Sloan asked.

Nerves knotted in my stomach as I glanced at him. "Yes. Do I usually drink something different?"

"No. You even have a favorite vineyard." He lifted a bottle, and I recognized the label. It was a wine I'd bought for special occasions. Once again, I felt something move through me at the thought that Cameron and I appreciated the same kind of wines.

"Does it stir any memories?" Sloan asked.

"No." He was testing me again, I realized. And since it was impossible to read his expression, I had no idea whether I'd passed or failed. Maybe it didn't matter. This whole masquerade was turning out to be much trickier than I'd anticipated. When Sloan handed the glass to me, I had to stop myself from drinking it all at once.

"Who are all these people?"

"A mix of business associates and family. James has told them about your temporary memory loss. They're a tough crowd, but they won't bite you. At least not in front of James." He spoke in a low tone only I could hear.

"I'll have something to look forward to then," I murmured.

When he chuckled, I felt some of my tension ease. And in spite of my earlier resolve that I should steer clear of Sloan, I was grateful for his presence at my side as he urged me toward the first group of people.

I recognized the man from the photos Pepper had included in her report even as Sloan said, "This is your cousin, Austin, and his fiancée Marcie Linton."

They made a striking couple, I thought. The tall blond Austin was the perfect foil for the petite and perky brunette. In stature and appearance, Austin took after his mother with his fair complexion, finely chiseled features and pale blue eyes. He looked like a cross between a Viking and a surfer.

According to Pepper, he had the reputation of a playboy and he gambled. In response to Sloan's introduction, he raised his glass in a toast. "Long time, no see, cousin. Congratulations. Uncle James has killed the fatted calf for you."

Marcie Linton sent him a quick frown. Austin didn't look overly happy to see me. Recalling Pepper's report, I thought I knew why. In my absence, he'd stepped into my shoes, and he probably wasn't too keen on stepping back out of them.

In response to Marcie's frown, he merely shrugged and took another sip of his drink. Marcie Linton was small, and she was even prettier than she'd been in her photos. Her slender body was encased in an ivory-colored linen dress, the perfect contrast to the jet-black hair that fell straight from a center part to below her shoulders and set off her delicate bone structure and porcelain-fair skin. Pepper had said that Cameron had hired her on as her personal assistant, and that when she and Austin had met, it had been love at first sight.

Giving up on Austin, Marcie sent me an apologetic smile and took my free hand in hers. "Don't pay Austin any heed. In your absence, your father has asked him to fill in for you, and he's done quite well. One of our new clients is here tonight—the Radcliffs." She gestured toward the far end of the room where James was seated in his wheelchair. "Austin signed them last week. I've assured him that you'll continue to need his help, at least until you're up to speed. Perhaps you could even put in a good word with your father."

"Sis, this isn't the time to talk business." I turned to face the man who'd joined us. His resemblance to Marcie was striking. He was taller, but under six feet. His features were more chiseled, the line of his chin stronger. His photos hadn't done him justice, either. In person, Hal Linton reminded me of George Clooney in *Oceans Eleven*, one cool charmer. I must have been staring because I didn't realize that he'd taken my hand from Marcie's until he raised it to his lips. "Welcome home, Cameron."

Sloan's grip on my elbow tightened fractionally. "This is Marcie's brother, Hal."

"I've missed you," Hal said as he finally released my hand.

The use of the singular pronoun had me wondering. I could sense undercurrents. Sloan was annoyed and Hal was aware of it. Did the two men have some history? Had Hal used the singular—"*I've* missed you?"—just to tick Sloan off, or did his use of it mean that he'd had some sort of relationship with Cameron?

Or was my imagination merely running wild again?

"I think we'd better talk to James," Sloan said and drew me away.

As we started down the length of the room, I said to Sloan in a low voice, "I thought my father said he was inviting the family. Who are all these people?"

When he replied, Sloan's voice was barely audible. "The older couple at the drink cart are the Lakewoods. They've done business with James ever since he took over the place from his father. The woman next to them is their daughter Rachel who is concerned about who will run the place after James. The Bolands haven't arrived yet. They have similar concerns and James will hold dinner for them."

I wanted to ask why James had invited these business associates, but Sloan continued, "The younger couple standing near your father is Jane and Sandy Radcliff."

I studied them. They must have been in their midthirties. "They breed horses in Texas, and thanks to you, they're interested in having us train three of their new colts. In your absence, Austin has done the paperwork, but you're responsible for bringing them on board." So Marcie hadn't told me the whole truth.

"Then I'm good at what I do?"

He glanced down at me. "You have a knack with people, and you have a lot of plans for expanding McKenzie Enterprises. The older man standing behind James's wheelchair is Doc Carter. He's widowed now, and he has a house within walking distance on the estate. He's been the family doctor ever since I can remember."

Doc Carter hadn't been in Pepper's report so I studied him now. He was medium height with a portly build and he wore wire-framed glasses. His mustache and the hair he had left were white. And when he threw back his head and laughed at something James said, he reminded me a bit of Santa Claus.

"James trusts him implicitly," Sloan was saying.

Who wouldn't trust Santa Claus, I thought.

"He and your mother traveled the year she was carrying you, and they took Doc Carter and his wife along. Lucky thing because you arrived a month early, and he had to make all the arrangements in a hospital in Switzerland."

As Sloan's words sank in, I very nearly stumbled. "I was born in Switzerland?"

"Yes. You were about a month old when they brought you back."

My head was spinning. Was it possible that Cameron had been passed off as James's biological daughter?

Didn't anyone here know that Cameron was adopted? Then I did stumble.

"Are you all right?" Sloan asked.

"Yes," I lied. My mind had jumped ahead to another explanation. What if Cameron hadn't been adopted? What if she and I were both James McKenzie's daughters—only I had been given up for adoption?

And that was ridiculous. My imagination really did run wild at times. Pepper had discovered adoption papers for both of us. Still...it would make a great story line for *Secrets*.

But this new information did leave open the possibility that no one besides James knew that Cameron was adopted.

"The woman to James's left is—"

"Is my Aunt Beatrice," I finished for him. The Snow Queen. "I met her when I arrived this morning."

Tonight, she wore a powdery-blue dress, outdated in its design. The filmy material flowed around her and I was once more reminded of a Tennessee Williams heroine—fragile, lovely, but clinging to a bygone day. But when she took my hand, I discovered her grip was surprisingly hard, and I recalled my earlier impression that she had strength that didn't appear on the surface.

"Welcome back, Cameron." Beatrice's voice was as ethereal as her appearance, and once more I couldn't read anything in her expression.

"Isn't it about time you paid your old father some attention, gal?" When I turned, James took my free hand and tugged it. With a smile, I leaned down and kissed his cheek.

"James has told us what happened to you," Jane

Radcliff said. "It must have been horrible to wake up in a strange place and not know who you are."

I met her eyes and smiled. Of all the strangers I'd met since I'd walked into the room, I sensed that she was sincere.

"Odd to think that you don't remember us," her husband, Sandy, said. "You're the reason that we decided to join forces with McKenzie Enterprises."

"She'll be up to speed in no time," James assured them.

"It's a miracle that she's back with us," Doc Carter commented. "Memory loss, even the kind that's caused by sudden trauma, can last for a long time. You look none the worse for wear," Doc Carter said. "But James wants me to see you tomorrow and check you out for myself."

I opened my mouth to protest, but Doc Carter continued. "It'll set James's mind at ease."

"Fine," I reluctantly agreed.

"The Bolands are late as usual," James said. "Sloan, while we're waiting, why don't you take Cameron for a stroll in the gardens? Maybe something there will trigger a memory."

I glanced at Sloan. "I'm sure he'd rather stay here."

"Nonsense," James declared. "He's wanted to get you alone since he brought you here. Beatrice and I can hold down the fort until dinner is served. Go." He shooed us with his hands. "You've been away from each other for over a month. You need some time alone together."

7

SLOAN TOOK MY HAND and led me through the nearest set of French doors. Once we'd crossed the terrace and started down the short flight of stairs to the garden, I asked, "Does my father always order people around like that?"

"Yeah."

I shot him a sideways glance. "You don't impress me as a man who's easily ordered around."

"I learned a long time ago to pick and choose my battles with James." When we reached the bottom of the steps, he guided me along a flagstone path which wound its way through a garden that had been laid out with meticulous care. Flowers of every color and size bordered the path, and their scents floated on the early-evening air.

"There are times when I go to the mat with him."

"Who wins?"

After a moment, he said, "Usually, I do. James is a smart man. He knows that when we disagree, there's a good reason, and he listens to what I have to say."

"Did he and Cameron butt heads often?"

He glanced at me then, and I could have sworn that there was a mocking glint in his eye.

"What?"

"It's odd hearing you refer to yourself in the third person."

He was sharp. I'd have to remember that. "I feel strange when I try to think of myself as Cameron McKenzie. It's going to take some getting used to."

Sloan steered me toward a wrought iron bench at the edge of the path. "We'll take a longer stroll another night when your ankle's had time to heal."

I started to protest, but he merely said, "Sit."

"You're as bad as my father is."

"Thanks. I'll take that as a compliment." He smiled as he sat down beside me, and I found myself wanting to smile back. Though I wouldn't call him charming, I was discovering that Sloan Campbell could be very disarming.

"Thank you for your help back there. It was…kind of you to fill me in on everyone."

"No problem."

I was very aware of the fact that Sloan had placed his arm along the back of the bench and that we were sitting close enough so that I could feel the heat of his body. As much to distract myself from that as out of curiosity, I asked, "Why was Dad so anxious to get us out of there?"

"The way I see it he's trying to accomplish three things at once. First, he's aware that tonight is a strain for you—meeting all these people that you don't remember."

His tone was neutral and he didn't look at me, but I sensed that he wasn't quite buying that yet.

"He's also showing the family and a select group of business associates that everything is back to normal on the McKenzie ranch. Cameron has returned, and the engagement is right back on track."

"*The* engagement? You mean ours?" I could hear a thread of panic in my voice.

Sloan shifted that intent gaze of his to mine and studied me for a moment. "Yes, our engagement. James's health has deteriorated in the past year. His heart attack last winter gave everyone a scare, and his arthritis is causing him to use his wheelchair more frequently."

"But the engagement is not back on track. Not really. I don't remember you."

"Enter Doc Carter. He's here tonight to assure everyone that he's going to work with you on recovering your memory. I imagine James will be emphasizing that while we're out here. By morning, the Lakewoods and the Bolands will be spreading the word to others."

I thought about it for a minute. "You said Dad was trying to accomplish three things at once. He doesn't want the evening to be too stressful for me, and he wants to reassure business associates. What's the third reason?"

"I suspect he's doing a bit of matchmaking."

I frowned at him. "Hasn't he already done that? We're engaged."

"But you don't remember me. James is providing us, not too subtly, with an opportunity to get reacquainted, Red. He's a master at manipulating people."

I was once more aware of how close we were on the bench. I could smell him above the scent of the flowers—soap and sun and something more elemental and very male.

I had to clear my throat. "And you're willing to go along with that even though you don't trust me?"

He raised his hand and touched the ends of my hair.

"I told you the jury's still out on the trust issue. Has anyone ever told you that you have honest eyes?"

"No." I barely got the word out. Every cell in my body was aware of his fingers as he tucked the strand of hair he held behind my ear. He was so close now that I could see his eyes were darker. They didn't remind me so much of fog as of the kind of dark-colored smoke that shoots up from a fire, and I found myself wondering what it would be like if he really touched me. I imagined the brush of those fingertips and the press of that hard palm against my shoulder, my arms, my...

I managed to clamp down on the images moving through my mind, but I couldn't prevent the arousal that started deep and spread as quickly as the ripples a stone would cause when it was tossed into a pond.

I drew in a deep breath and let it out, wishing I could just as easily get rid of the heat that was flooding through me. I reminded myself of my mission. James might have had his agenda for sending Sloan and me into the garden, but he'd also given me an opportunity that I couldn't afford to ignore. "Why did I run away?"

Sloan studied me for a minute.

"Or why do you think I ran away?"

"The usual reason. You needed time to think."

"About what? Was I having second thoughts about the wedding?"

"Perhaps."

I couldn't read anything in his expression. He was still playing with the ends of my hair.

"Were you worried that I'd change my mind?"

"No. The whole wedding thing was your idea. You proposed to me."

That was news. "Dad said we argued the night before I went away. What about?"

Once again, he hesitated for just a beat. "If I told you, you'd only have my version. I think you should wait until you get your memory back."

Once again, I caught something in his eyes—just a hint of mockery. "You don't think I really lost my memory, do you?"

"The thought has crossed my mind that you're faking it." He hadn't dropped his hand from my hair, and he seemed to be even closer. I had to struggle to keep my voice steady. "Why do you think that Cameron—that I would come back here faking memory loss?"

"It all goes back to why you ran away in the first place. As I said, my best guess was that you were having second thoughts about the wedding. You needed some time alone to think, so you took off. The memory loss story gives you a chance to come back without having to admit that you ran away. You always hated to admit you were wrong, or worse still, make a fool of yourself."

The fact that he could believe my sister capable of such duplicity intrigued me. Might I have tried the same kind of masquerade in her situation? Then it occurred to me. Wasn't the impersonation I was engaged in just as daring? Perhaps Cameron and I weren't as different as I'd originally thought.

"Would I really do something like that?"

"Oh, yes. You like to play games, and you always like to win."

As he continued to play with the ends of my hair, I realized that the bigger question was why would any woman be having second thoughts about marrying a man like Sloan Campbell? Or was I just blinded by the fact that I was so attracted to him?

"You know me very well then?"

"I've known you pretty much all your life. I was born and raised here. My mother died when I was a baby. My father had the same job that I do now—he was James's right-hand man running the stables and training horses. They were best friends until my father ran away with James's first wife, Sarah."

Pepper had written briefly about this story in her report, but it was different hearing it from Sloan. I found my heart going out to the little boy. I reached out and took his hand. "How old were you?"

"Two. But you needn't feel sorry for me. James never harbored any resentment against me. He took me in and raised me as if I were his own. He remarried two years later, and you were born two years after that."

I did the math quickly in my head. Sloan was about six years older than I was. That made him thirty-one.

"What happened? Did your father ever contact you?"

Sloan shook his head. "James hired a P.I. to trace them, but he wasn't successful. My guess is that he wasn't much interested in tracking them down. I hired a P.I. five years ago to look into it, but the trail was cold by then."

I continued to study him. There was so much I wanted to know. I wanted to ask him why he'd left the ranch five years ago, but I wouldn't have any way of knowing about that. The memory loss thing was tricky—especially with someone who thought I might be faking it.

"Penny for your thoughts," Sloan said.

When I didn't immediately answer, he ran the pad of

his thumb over my bottom lip. "I'll share mine for free. I've been thinking of how soft your mouth is."

His gesture and the words had my mouth trembling, and I felt a flare of something deep inside me that was raw and stunning. He was going to kiss me.

I should have said something. There were so many reasons for not kissing Sloan again, I could have made a list. But right now I couldn't seem to summon up even one reason, not while his breath whispered over my skin, not while those dark eyes were looking into mine.

The alarm bells ringing in my mind warned me to move away, but my body was no longer taking orders from my brain. Or perhaps my brain was no longer capable of giving any intelligent kind of orders. Bottom line, I wanted Sloan to kiss me again.

But he wasn't moving. He was waiting for me.

Just one more time, I told myself. Didn't I have a right to know if it would be as intense an experience as the first time? My curiosity would be satisfied and then I would move on. That was the problem with forbidden fruit—one taste was just never enough. I leaned forward.

The first brush of his lips against mine was light, exactly as it had been before. And not exactly what I wanted. Still, I felt the soft caress right down to my toes. All of my senses were immediately heightened. I felt the firmness of his hand, those strong fingers moving up and down on the nape of my neck while his thumb rested at the hollow of my throat. A mix of anticipation and longing moved through me. I could hear my pulse hammer, feel it beat in a frantic rhythm against his thumb.

His mouth brushed over my lips, slowly, as if he wanted to commit them to memory. The movement was so lazy, so mesmerizing. I'd never been so aware of a man before, never experienced this kind of intensity in a man's touch. I wanted to simply melt into him.

As if he could read my mind, he put his arm around me and drew me close until every hard angle and plane of his body was pressed against mine. Then I *was* melting. I felt parts of myself slipping away. I tried to say his name, but all I heard was a sound, part sigh, part moan. He took my bottom lip between his teeth and bit it sharply, then used his tongue to soothe the ache. Explosions of pleasure shot through me, as he drew my lip into his mouth and sucked hard on it. Desire twisted tight in my center.

My fingers dug into his shoulders, and as if he were waiting for that particular response, Sloan finally pressed his mouth fully to mine. I knew the sensation of instant fire—I couldn't tell whether it came from me or him or both of us. But in that moment it was clear this man could make me want more, demand more than I ever had before.

My tongue met his, seeking, searching. His mouth was…paradise. The rich, dark taste of him was so enticing, so absorbing, I could have explored it forever. Jolts of hot pleasure coursed through me, and I needed more. I felt his muscles so hard beneath my palms, and the sound he made deep in his throat told me he was feeling at least something of what I was. I pressed myself against him, felt his arms tighten around me.

Passion had never tasted this ripe, this dark before.

Desire had never been so sharp, so overpowering that it hurt.

I was so caught up in it, so lost in the moment and

in the man that I wasn't even aware when we were interrupted.

I just knew that Sloan drew away, and I nearly shivered at the abrupt loss of heat. He didn't release his grip on me. If he had, I think I would have slid right off the bench. Instead, he settled my head against his shoulder, holding me as he spoke to whomever was standing behind me on the path.

"We'll be right in."

I heard the words, but it took my mind a few beats before I could make meaning out of them. We were being called into dinner. I had to get it together. More than that, I had to face Sloan. Gathering all my strength, I lifted my head from his shoulder and drew away.

I met his eyes, and he met mine. Neither of us spoke for a moment, and I wished that I could tell what he was thinking. What does one say to a man who's just turned you into a puddle of lust? I was a writer. I should have had lots of words and phrases at my command, but what popped out of my mouth surprised me. "I can't imagine why I would have run away from you."

The look he gave me was enigmatic. "You don't know me yet."

A SHORT DISTANCE AWAY, a shadow silently moved among other shadows in the garden, watching as the man and woman rose and moved back toward the patio.

She was back. Just thinking the words had the anger building. It wasn't fair. It wasn't right. Everything had been going so smoothly. She'd been eliminated. Finally, justice had been accomplished.

But she was back. Fury erupted. Then ruthlessly the

emotion was shoved down. Anger never solved anything. That had been a lesson learned at an early age.

Anger never changed what was. It wouldn't change the fact that she'd returned. Speculating on how was a waste of time. The plan had been perfect…. But the only thing that mattered now was a new plan.

All that mattered was that she had to be eliminated…again. This time there would be no mistake. And then everything would be perfect.

8

I BARELY BIT BACK A SIGH as two servants carried in yet
another set of platters from the kitchen. The dining
room was every bit as cavernous as the main parlor had
been. Three crystal chandeliers hung from the ceiling,
and we sat at a huge oak table that looked as if it had
been used by Don Roberto Montega, the man who'd
built the hacienda. There were small vases of flowers at
intervals along the table.

Instead of four or five courses, Elena and another
woman had carried in platters heaped with rare roast
beef, chicken in a delicate lemon caper sauce and bowls
of salads, grilled vegetables and warm bread. I'd eaten
in self-defense because I couldn't very well talk when
my mouth was full, could I? Beatrice, who sat to my left,
for the most part ignored me and played the gracious
hostess, making sure that the meal unfolded smoothly.

Austin was drinking quite a bit. He would have had
even more if Beatrice hadn't signaled one of the servants
to stop refilling his wineglass. She done it in such a
subtle and smooth way that I assumed it was something
she'd had to do frequently in the past. My cousin still
wasn't trying to hide the fact that he resented my
presence, and he hadn't said a word to me all during

dinner. Marcie tried to compensate for his behavior by inviting me to go riding with them the following afternoon. She and Austin were sure that I would want to reacquaint myself with my horse, Lace Ribbons.

Because I felt a bit sorry for her, I might have agreed anyway, but Doc Carter said, "I think that would be a good idea, Cameron. You love riding. The more you familiarize yourself with Cameron's routines, the quicker your memory might come back."

"Fine." I aimed a smile in Marcie's direction. But I couldn't help feeling that I was being maneuvered by her just as surely as James had maneuvered me earlier. I promised myself that I would get away from all of them in the morning and do a little exploring on my own.

Then because I had Dr. Carter's attention for the moment, I said, "I'm trying to get a feel for what my last day here was like—I mean before I left. Do you remember seeing me that day? Did we talk?"

Dr. Carter studied me for a moment. "That's good. I think it might be a very good idea to try and put together that day."

"Did you see me? Were you here that day?"

He shook his head. "If I remember correctly, it was a Monday, and I spent the day in my backyard working on my putting. Since I retired, I had a putting green put in, and if the weather permits, I'm out there every day. Golf has become my obsession since my wife passed away. But I did walk over here in the late afternoon to check on James, of course. And we had our usual chess game." He smiled at me. "And if I played the way I usually do, I probably lost. Does that help at all?"

"No." I could give Pepper the information, but if Doc

Carter lived alone, it meant that he didn't have an alibi. Not that I could believe that Santa Claus could have had something to do with my sister's disappearance.

He patted my hand. "Patience. Your memory will return when you least expect it."

Sloan. The moment that Doc Carter turned away, I cut a piece of roast beef off and pushed it around my plate. The evening would have been stressful enough anyway, but my reaction to Sloan's kiss had made it even more so because I couldn't put it out of my mind.

I shouldn't have allowed it to happen. I could have prevented it. But all the should haves and could haves didn't change the fact that I hadn't followed my plan to steer clear of Sloan Campbell. Now I was in trouble, and I had a hunch that it was going to get worse.

The good news was that he'd been seated at the far end of the table from me with James, the Bolands and the Radcliffs. I understood the strategy of the arrangement. Sloan was able to finally spend some time with clients, and I was isolated from them, surrounded by family and projecting an image of normalcy.

But that hadn't made it any easier to digest my food. I sliced off another piece of roast beef and rearranged its position on my plate.

The dining room walls were an ochre color and paintings by the same artist whose work had been displayed in the main parlor also hung here. There was something about the stark simplicity of them that appealed to me.

"Do you know who the artist is?" I asked Doc Carter.

He gave me a searching look. Of all the people in my immediate vicinity, I liked him the best. There was an easy geniality about him, a kindness in his eyes, and not

once during the meal had he pressed me about my
memory loss, other than to suggest I go riding with
Marcie and Austin.

"Do they look at all familiar?" he asked.

I shook my head. "I assume they're scenes of the
ranch."

"They are. Your mother painted all of them," he said.

My mother. He had to be talking about James's
second wife, Elizabeth. My gaze returned to the painting
that hung on the wall above Beatrice's head. It was a
landscape that must have been painted from one of the
bluffs where I'd stood earlier in the day to get my bird's-
eye view of the hacienda.

I recalled my earlier suspicion that James had passed
Cameron off as his biological daughter. Had my sister
been kept just as ignorant of her real background as I
had been? The possibility stirred something inside of
me. Did we have more in common than I'd thought?

I turned to Doc Carter intending to find out more
information about my mother, but he was talking to
Jane Radcliff.

"Elizabeth was a very talented painter."

I turned to Beatrice. It was the first she'd spoken to
me since we'd sat down at the table. Not that she'd
spoken much more to Marcie and Austin. She was a
quiet, self-contained woman.

"Did she ever sell any of them?" I asked.

"If she hadn't passed away, Elizabeth would have had
a show in a gallery in San Francisco," Beatrice said. "It
was all arranged, but after her death, James canceled the
show. He couldn't bear to part with any of her work."

"What did she…my mother die of?" I asked.

There was a beat of silence, then Beatrice replied, her voice even softer, "After she and James returned from Europe with you, she began to have frequent bouts of illness and depression. Each one left her weaker than the last. The doctors couldn't seem to find anything wrong with her."

"It sounds like postpartum depression." We'd just run a story line on *Secrets* in which one of the lead ingenues had nearly killed her child. "It could have been treated."

"It was. Doc Carter tried everything," Beatrice assured me. "Your father spared no expense, and for a while, the drugs seemed to work. She even began painting again."

Whatever else she might have told me was forestalled by James, who tapped on his wineglass until he had everyone's attention. "We'll have coffee and after-dinner drinks in the parlor. I have an important announcement to make."

I rose and followed the procession that was making its way back to the parlor. But as soon as I stepped into the hallway, Hal Linton, who hadn't spoken a word to me during dinner, took my hand and turned me around to face him.

"I have to speak with you in private," he said.

I'd thought that Beatrice was behind us, but over Hal's shoulder, I saw that she was headed down the hallway in the opposite direction. A quick glance over my own shoulder told me that Austin and Marcie had already entered the parlor leaving Hal and me alone.

As Hal drew me into an alcove, I had the distinct impression that I had been manipulated again. And I was getting tired of it.

Hal raised my hand and pressed his lips to it. "I've missed you. When can I see you?"

I tried to draw my hand away, but he tightened his grip. "You're seeing me right now."

He studied me intently. "I need to see you alone. You can't have forgotten what happened between us the night before you left."

The implication of what he was saying had my head spinning. What had been my sister's relationship with this man?

"I've been so worried about you. When you disappeared so abruptly, I thought he'd gone into a jealous rage and done something to you."

A sliver of ice worked its way up my spine. This time I managed to get my hand free. "What are you talking about?"

"Sloan. He's incredibly possessive of you, and he discovered us in the garden that night. We were kissing, and he demanded that you go with him. Everyone knew that you quarreled. And he has a terrible temper." He had his hands on my shoulders and was drawing me closer. "Do you know what it's been like for me, worrying about you for weeks? And then tonight, seeing you come into the parlor, sitting across from you at the table and not being able to touch you. Please—"

"No." I put my hands on Hal's chest and gave him a shove that sent him back against the wall of the alcove.

Behind me came Sloan's even tone. "James is waiting for you, Cameron."

My legs felt like rubber as I turned and walked out of the alcove.

"Can you explain what just happened back there?" I asked Sloan softly as we walked side-by-side down the hall.

"Looked pretty obvious to me," Sloan said. "Old Hal made a pass and you nixed it."

What was obvious to me was that Sloan didn't seem to care a bit. There hadn't been a trace of anger or annoyance in either his actions or his voice. Didn't he care if someone made a pass at his fiancée? How could he have kissed me as he had in the garden and then been so cool when he'd found me extricating myself from another man's arms?

And I couldn't forget what Hal had said. His version of the argument that Sloan and Cameron had had on the night before she disappeared differed from James's version. And Sloan had refused to talk about it at all.

When I entered the parlor, James was sitting near the fireplace, pouring champagne into flutes and the bartender was passing them out to the guests. He'd said he had an announcement to make. Had he and Sloan closed some kind of important deal over dinner?

Sloan took two glasses from the tray he was offered and handed one to me.

"I mentioned an announcement," James said, "and I don't think it should come as a surprise to anyone. My daughter's disappearance was a harsh reminder of how little time there is and how quickly it passes. As a result, I've decided that her wedding to Sloan, which would have taken place in September, will take place here on Friday evening."

Friday was the day after tomorrow. I nearly dropped the glass of champagne I was holding. I would have if

Sloan hadn't reached out and steadied my hand. "He can't mean that," I said.

"He means it all right," Sloan confirmed in a low tone. "He's a sneaky, manipulating bastard, and it's just like him to pull something like this."

"I don't have the patience to wait any longer," James continued. "And I don't think Sloan does, either. Since I've known all of you from the start of McKenzie Enterprises, you're invited. The ceremony will be at five in the chapel, and we'll have a small celebration afterward." Then he raised his glass in the air. "To the happy couple."

"If you don't do something," I said in an undertone to Sloan, "I will."

"Be my guest."

I had the distinct and annoying suspicion that Sloan was enjoying this. That only increased my determination.

I strode forward until I was standing directly in front of James, who was flanked on one side by Beatrice and on the other by Doc Carter. I kept my eyes on James. "I can't do this. I don't remember Sloan. I need more time."

James took my hand and squeezed it. "Humor an old man, Cammy. Doc Carter is convinced that all you need is a bit more time. Everyone here will help you to get your memory back by Friday. Sloan will see that you get a grand tour of the estate first thing tomorrow. You'll see. You'll be back to normal in no time."

I turned back to Sloan, still hoping that he'd join me in protest, but he seemed perfectly okay with the announcement. In fact from the look he gave me, I was sure he'd been anticipating it. I couldn't believe that he was letting James do this.

James squeezed my hand again and drew me down closer. "Please. You and Sloan were meant for each other. Trust me and do this for me. The future of the McKenzie ranch depends on you."

Sloan was right. James was a manipulative and wily old man, and he'd staged this on purpose in front of clients. In fact, I was sure that's why the Bolands and the Lakewoods and the Radcliffs had been invited. I could have put up a bigger fight if there'd just been the family. And I would have, I told myself.

"Cammy?" James said.

"Yes. Okay." I told myself I had two days to talk James or Sloan or both of them out of this. In a soap opera story line that was plenty of time. And I was good at inventing new plot twists. If all else failed I could just say no when I was at the altar. I couldn't be forced to marry anyone. Could I?

"To the bride and groom and to the future of McKenzie Enterprises."

"Hear, hear!"

As we all raised our glasses and sipped champagne, I scanned the faces of Cameron's family. From what I could see, only James seemed happy with the surprise announcement.

"To the bride," Sloan said, slipping his hand into mine.

As everyone drank again, I turned to find both amusement and challenge in his eyes. I promised myself that I was going to figure him out.

If it killed me?

9

THE MOMENT HE GOT BACK to the carriage house, Sloan slipped out of his jacket and pulled off his boots. Then he grabbed a beer out of the refrigerator and walked out onto the deck that offered a view of both the stables and the hacienda. Settling himself in a cushioned chair, he propped his feet up on the railing and took a long swallow of beer.

Taking a half hour to sit down, put his feet up and review the events of the day was a habit he'd developed in his late teens—minus the beer, of course. Sometimes he turned on the CD player, but tonight he wanted the quiet. He had a lot to sort through. And it all centered on Red.

He'd called her that at first because he wasn't going to call her Cameron. And he had figured it might annoy her or at the very least throw her a bit off balance. But the name seemed to somehow fit her.

And he'd kissed her again. The kiss hadn't been a test this time. He wasn't a man who felt there was anything to be gained by lying to himself. He'd kissed her again because he wanted to. And because he hadn't been able to resist finding out if she'd have the same effect she'd had on him the first time.

And now he knew. He wanted Red with an intensity that he'd never felt for any other woman.

It hadn't done much good telling himself that she might be a lying little, fortune-hunting imposter. The fact remained that he wanted more from her than a kiss. And there was no use lecturing himself that he shouldn't take more. No use at all pretending that he wouldn't take more. Because he would.

Hell, he nearly had.

His gaze dropped to the garden below. He thought he could make out the bench where they'd kissed just a few hours ago. If someone hadn't interrupted them, he would have made love to her right there. He was skilled enough, and she'd been aroused enough. It would have been wild, and crazy...and very dangerous. Everything else aside, he certainly hadn't gone to James's little dinner party with condoms at the ready. He hadn't been tempted to run a risk like that since he was a teenager in the grip of almost-terminal hormones.

Red could certainly push his buttons all right. And why not? Any man would be tempted by the passion that was simmering just below the surface. One taste of her and all he could think of was having her beneath him, of losing himself inside of her.

That didn't bother him as much as the fact that when he'd seen her in Hal Linton's arms, jealousy had sliced through him right to the bone. He hadn't felt that when he'd seen Hal kissing Cameron in the garden five weeks ago.

Sloan took another swallow of beer. The other thing worrying him was that he was coming to like Red. He thought of the way she'd marched across the parlor to face down James. Even in his wheelchair, the old man had been able to glower at her at eye level. David taking on Goliath, he thought with a smile. And there was that shove she'd given Linton. It had sent him tumbling back against the wall.

Not only was he beginning to like her, he was also more and more intrigued by her. She was dead set against marrying him. Before the party broke up, she'd taken him aside to try and talk him into persuading James to postpone the wedding. His gaze shifted to the hacienda and the light he could see in James's suite. She was there with him now, trying to plead her case.

Why? If she was the fortune hunter he suspected her of being, why wasn't she happy about the wedding? She had to figure that in two days, James would sign his new will and she'd be a millionairess.

And just what kind of a game was James playing? Had he moved up the wedding because of what he'd said in the parlor or was he involved in something deeper?

He couldn't help wondering what part Cameron might be playing in all of this. Leaning his head back against the chair, Sloan closed his eyes and tried to sort through what he knew and what he didn't.

Fact number one, Cameron had disappeared five weeks ago, and everyone including himself had believed that she'd taken off because she was having second thoughts about the wedding.

He knew for a fact that she had been. Right after he'd caught her kissing Hal Linton in the gardens, they'd argued. He'd told her that it wasn't the kind of behavior he would accept after they were married, and she'd blown up, told him she'd act whatever way she pleased. She'd threatened to call the wedding off, and he'd told her to go ahead.

But there hadn't been any real passion in the fight.

Cameron had been angry, but not at him. She'd been angry with her father, angry that he wouldn't leave the land to her because she was a woman. As a result, their quarrel was more like an argument he would have had with Cameron years ago—the kind that a brother and sister might have.

And that was the crux of the problem. As the wedding date drew closer, both of them were realizing what they would be giving up if they went through with the marriage.

They'd have the land, and he had no doubt that they'd eventually have children. But there would never be anything between them but the kind of love that exists between siblings or good friends.

Opening his eyes, Sloan looked at the hacienda and the stables beyond drenched in moonlight. What he and Cameron shared was a passion for this land, but not for each other. That was why Cameron had asked him to marry her. He wasn't sure whether it had been entirely her idea or if James had proposed it. But he knew why Cameron had gone along with it. She'd been scared when James had had the heart attack. She'd been angry then, too, because James was not going to leave the estate entirely in the hands of a woman. In the will he'd made out after the heart attack, he'd left it to a board of directors he'd personally selected. The board would make all the business decisions. Cameron would be provided for, but she'd have little control in the daily running of the ranch.

Sloan rubbed a hand over his face. The old man knew how to push the right buttons to get what he wanted. If Cameron was a game player, she'd come by it honestly.

Wasn't that why he'd left five years ago—because he'd wanted to decide on his own what he wanted in life? He hadn't wanted to spend his life working for James McKenzie. He'd wanted to run his own ranch.

The proposition that Cameron had made to him at the Derby would allow him to do just that. They would be equal partners. He would be in charge of the horses and the ranch. She would be in charge of client relations and recruiting new business. They'd both have what they wanted. All they had to do was get married.

He swept his gaze over the estate again, lingering first on the stables and then on the hacienda itself. This was what he'd always wanted, from the time he was a kid. He'd accepted Cameron's proposal because of this.

And she wasn't the only one who'd been having second thoughts five weeks ago. He had been, too, and he'd been secretly relieved that she'd taken off and given them both a little time to think.

That brought up fact number two. Red's appearance raised the question of whether or not Cameron's disappearance was voluntary or if someone else had played a hand in it. To answer that question he was going to have to spend a lot of time with the woman he was calling Red.

And that was going to lead to…having her. He was not going to fool himself about that. In spite of those honest eyes, she was a liar and possibly a fortune hunter. Worst-case scenario, she might be a pawn in some deeper game that James McKenzie was playing. But even that possibility was not going to make a difference.

Realizing that his thoughts had come full circle, Sloan reached down for his bottle and discovered that it was empty. He took his feet off the railing, but he didn't go into the house for a very long time.

WHEN I FINALLY LET MYSELF into Cameron's room, my stomach was in knots, I had a headache pounding behind my eyes and I very badly wanted to kick something. The room was dark except for the moonlight pouring through the balconied windows on either side of the bed. I moved to one of the tables and flipped on a lamp.

Hannibal was sprawled across my pillows glaring at me through narrowed eyes.

I fisted my hands on my hips. "You don't want to mess with me. I've had a very bad night."

The cat's expression didn't change. He didn't even blink.

"Okay," I said. "You don't like me and I don't like you. But I need some sleep, and I intend to sleep in this bed—not curled up on the foot like a…like a…" Cat, I finished silently.

It occurred to me then that I was taking out my frustration on the poor cat when what I really wanted to do was strangle Sloan.

With a frustrated sigh, I strode to the cabinet and got out treats for both of us. Luckily my sister kept a generous supply. After tossing a couple of cat tidbits at Hannibal, I walked to the window and took a bite of chocolate. I'd learned after the guests had left that Sloan didn't live in the main house. He lived in the carriage house beyond the stables. I could just make it out in the moonlight.

I'd never met a man like him before. Not that I hadn't had to deal with some difficult men in my life. Male soap stars whose careers can depend on what twist a story line takes are not the easiest people to deal with. But at least their ego-driven motivations were always clear. Sloan Campbell's were a mystery to me.

He hadn't seemed at all upset when he'd found me with Hal Linton. What had his relationship with my sister been? Was their marriage strictly a business arrangement? Or was it one of those "modern" deals where, after the knot was tied, the two individuals went their separate ways? Sloan hadn't impressed me as that kind of a man. And I hoped that my sister wasn't that kind of a woman.

I turned back to Hannibal. "Maybe I'm just too much of a romantic. And I'm not rich." My parents had been able to raise me in a very comfortable house, provide me with a good education, private schools and nice vacations. But they weren't rich, rich. Cameron was. I'd already discovered that there was a world of difference between the contents of my closet and hers. And Sloan Campbell would be rich when he married her and James deeded the estate and the business to the two of them.

I knew enough, had lived long enough to know that the rich *were* different. I turned back to look out over the gardens and the stables. Maybe inheriting a place like this was motive enough to settle for an arranged marriage. Perhaps in Cameron's shoes, I would have agreed to it. I now knew from experience how persuasive James could be.

But Sloan? Somehow, I couldn't picture him allowing anyone to push him into something like that. Not even for money. Unless he was doing it for James. James McKenzie had raised him, and I could see that Sloan loved him like a father.

I frowned and pressed my hands against the headache that was beginning to drum at my temples. Even if Sloan had originally agreed to the marriage out of love for James, that didn't explain why he was agreeing to the rushed wedding now.

Hadn't the man told me that he picked his battles with James, and that when he went to the mat, he usually was able to make the old man see reason? So why had he allowed us to be manipulated into this wedding on Friday?

He couldn't possibly want it any more than I did. Good heavens, the man thought I'd run away and now was faking amnesia just to save face. Agreeing to the marriage in the first place was one thing. But why in the world would he want to go through with it when Cameron was so clearly ambivalent? His acquiescence contradicted everything that my instincts told me about the man.

Unless my instincts were being clouded by the fact that he attracted me so strongly and on such an elemental level. Or unless there were facts that I didn't know.

Turning, I walked to the bed. I needed to sleep on it. I found that sleeping on problems—knots that I couldn't untie in a plot—often solved them. Hopefully, my unconscious mind would sort through everything, and in the morning I would have a fresh perspective.

Hannibal was still sitting on his throne of pillows at the head of the bed.

"Okay," I muttered to him. "I'll share, but I'm not sleeping at the foot of the bed. You're going to have to move over."

After shooting me a bland look, he began to lazily clean one of his paws. Hoping it wasn't a threat to scratch me, I circled around the bed. It was only then that I noticed my duffel bag. I'd brought it up when Elena had first taken me to the room. It was sitting on the bench at the foot of the bed, but I was sure that I'd left it in Cameron's closet. I was equally sure that the zipper had been closed, and it was open now.

I reached in and pulled out my wallet. A quick check assured me that my money was still there. But the bills had been pulled out and stuffed back in carelessly. The few clothes that I'd brought had been rifled through.

Ice formed a hard little ball in my stomach as I sank down onto the bench. Someone had come into my room and searched my duffel bag and wallet, and they didn't care if I found out. Somehow that frightened me more than the fact that someone had searched my things.

Who?

The answer to that was anyone could have done it sometime during the evening with the possible exception of James. After everyone else had left, he'd asked me to accompany him to his suite. I'd gone because I'd thought I might be able to reason with him and get him to change his mind about the wedding on Friday. But he'd looked tired when we reached his room. And fragile. For the first time I'd realized that the evening had been as much of a strain for him as it had been for me.

I frowned down at the wallet that I was still holding so tightly that my fingers had begun to ache. Even Sloan would have had an opportunity to come up here and search through my things before he'd returned to the carriage house.

Deliberately, I willed my hands to relax and set the wallet down on the bench beside me. Why was it that my mind constantly circled back to Sloan Campbell?

He'd been the one person to express openly his doubts about my being Cameron.

But that wasn't the only reason I couldn't stop thinking about him. The man had a grip on me, mind and body, that I'd never experienced before. If I wasn't careful, he might turn into an obsession.

I forced myself to think about what had happened as if it were a plot line I was developing. Character—who could have done this? And then motivation—why? Why usually pointed to who.

Anyone could have slipped in here. Austin, for example. He didn't like me and had made no effort to hide it. Plus, my return meant that he had to step down from a job that he might have grown attached to. I knew from Pepper's report that Austin was only a year older than Cameron, so they'd grown up in the same house together. Had they always been in competition with one another? That might explain why he hadn't bothered to hide his animosity toward me from James.

In spite of his mother's intervention, Austin had been drinking pretty heavily at dinner. That might explain why he'd been so careless about looking through my things. Or he may have wanted me to know that he'd searched them.

Then there were the Lintons—Marcie and Hal. What was their stake in all of this? Marcie had been friendly enough, but if she hadn't lied about who had signed the Radcliffs as clients, she'd certainly stretched the truth. Hal had been a bit too friendly, and it was clear from what Cole and Pepper had found out that he had an agenda. The land developers he represented wanted that strip of McKenzie land along the Pacific. Romancing the heiress apparent could be his way of furthering that agenda.

And I couldn't shake the thought that Austin and Marcie had helped Hal Linton get me alone after dinner. It had been too neat a maneuver to have been an accident.

Marcie was engaged to Austin. Had Hal made a move on my sister with the hope that if he could prevent the marriage, then James might decide to leave the estate to Austin…? I was going to have to find out more about Cameron's relationship with Hal. Did he have his sights set on becoming Mr. Cameron McKenzie or was he playing a deeper game?

Any one of the possible scenarios I'd just cooked up would work beautifully in *Secrets*, but in real life…?

Rising, I started to pace back and forth at the foot of the bed. I needed to find out more about these people. And I could do that. I was a writer, and I knew how to do research. First thing in the morning I'd call Pepper and give her the information I'd gotten from Elena so she could check out alibis, and I'd ask her to check out the Lintons more thoroughly. And I'd talk again to Elena. Servants knew a lot about the families they served, and she might have more objective insights than I was likely to get anywhere else.

Who else could I interview? Doc Carter. He was going to drop by tomorrow after lunch to see me, and I'd use my time with him to gather more information. And then I'd go riding with Marcie and Austin and gather more data from the "horse's mouth" so to speak.

I jumped at the sound of my cell phone, then grinned. It had to be Pepper. Was this ESP or what? She was the only one who had the number for my new cell. I pulled it out of the duffel and pressed the button to take the incoming call.

The voice was soft and tinny sounding.

"You should never have come back. You weren't supposed to come back. Ever. Leave now or you'll share the fate of the other mistresses of the Hacienda Montega."

I wasn't aware of it when my knees gave out. The next thing I knew I was sitting on the floor staring down at the cell phone in my hand. There was a lump blocking my throat, I was shivering, and even my brain cells seemed numb.

In spite of that, questions filtered through. What had been the fate of the mistresses of this house? And had my sister already shared it?

10

"GOOD MORNING."

I had to swallow disappointment when I saw Marcie Linton at the foot of the stairs. I smiled and said, "You're an early riser."

"Not usually. But I was hoping to get a chance to talk to you…alone."

"Sure," I said. I had to admire her strategy. I'd gotten up at six-thirty and managed a quick shower and an even quicker phone call to Pepper in the hopes of doing the same thing with Elena.

"We usually have breakfast in here." Marcie led me down a short hallway.

There was an energy about the petite brunette that I admired. But I didn't quite trust her. Of course, my perspective on her could have been tainted by the fact that she reminded me of the ingenue on *Secrets* who had put Mallory Carstairs in the coma. But Cameron had hired her, I reminded myself.

"You'll be my new best friend if you can find me coffee," I said.

Marcie laughed. "It's Elena that's your new best friend then. She keeps fresh coffee in the breakfast room all morning. There's also tea because that's what Beatrice prefers."

"You seem familiar with the routine."

She glanced over her shoulder at me. "Austin and I have been spending more time here since you…went away."

We stepped into a bright sunny space with terrace doors that opened out to the gardens and the pool. The room was considerably smaller than the formal parlor and dining room that I'd been in last night, but the dark oak buffet and table, though they were built on a large scale, fit easily into the room. Unable to resist, I ran my hand over the intricate carving on the buffet. "It's beautiful."

"These pieces were shipped over from Spain as part of the Countess Montega's dowry," Marcie explained as she selected a mug from the buffet, filled it and handed it to me.

I took my first sip and waited for that first jolt of caffeine to spread through my system. My night's sleep—what there'd been of it—had been plagued by strange dreams and turf battles with Hannibal. The cat had actually nudged me right onto the floor at one point.

"Much of the original furniture and all of the art was sold off at one time or another over the years," Marcie continued, "but the larger-scale pieces were either too hard to remove or less marketable at the time. Silas McKenzie was lucky in that respect."

She was not only at home here, I thought, but she was also very much up to speed on the history of the house. I sipped more coffee. She was being very nice to me, but I didn't doubt for a minute that she had an agenda. Charming or at least disarming me had to be at the top of her list.

"What would you like for breakfast? I can highly recommend Elena's huevos rancheros."

"That's fine," I said.

"Good. I'll be right back." She disappeared through a swinging door.

Alone for the moment, I admired the roses that filled a large cut crystal vase. Everywhere I went in this house, there seemed to be flowers. Beatrice's doing. Then I stepped out onto the sunlit terrace. I hadn't been out of the house since Sloan had brought me back here the day before—except for that short stroll in the garden last night. And I wasn't going to think about that. Or about the kiss.

Pushing the thought and the temptation away, I crossed slowly to the edge of the terrace. The early-morning sun was already warm, and the air carried the scent of mown grass, flowers and horses. A far cry from the scents I was used to as a city girl.

From the terrace, I had a view of one of the riding rings, and I spotted Sloan immediately. He was already at work with one of the horses. Saturn.

He turned at almost the same instant that I saw him. I could have sworn that my heart stuttered. He was at least three football fields away, and still, something not unlike a little electric shock moved through me. Then my heart stuttered again when he leaped onto the horse, urged him to take the fence and rode toward me.

I walked down the steps of the terrace and on one of the paths to meet him. It wasn't wise. This was not someone I should be having these feelings for. But I couldn't seem to help myself. As he grew closer, I once again marveled at the beauty of the way man and horse moved together as one.

Sloan was wearing sunglasses, so I couldn't see his eyes until he dismounted and lifted them to rest on the top of his head. It was against all logic, but I was ridiculously happy just to see him again. So I smiled.

He put a finger under my chin tilting it up. Then he just studied me for a minute. Once again, I felt the intensity of his touch right down to my toes.

"You didn't sleep well last night, Red," he said.

"Did the bags under my eyes give me away?"

The corners of his mouth twitched. "You might say that. If you want to postpone the grand tour I'm supposed to give you, we can do it tomorrow."

"No. I want to see the ranch." That was the truth, but not the whole truth. The whole truth was that I felt safer now that he was here than I had since I'd gotten that phone call last night. I knew it was a probably a mistake, a big one, but I couldn't seem to help myself. I wanted very much to trust Sloan Campbell.

Saturn whinnied and pushed his nose into my shoulder. Sloan grabbed my arm to steady me. Then Saturn nudged me again, harder.

Laughing, I patted the horse's neck. "What's the matter, you beauty?"

"Looks like he wants his share of attention," Sloan said.

As I continued to stroke the horse, I said on impulse, "I'd love to ride him. May I?"

Sloan's eyes narrowed. "Don't let his looks fool you. He can be difficult to control."

"That would be the challenge, wouldn't it? My…" I caught myself just in time. I'd been about to tell Sloan about Dandelion's Pride, one of the horses that I'd ridden in several shows.

"You were saying?" Sloan asked.

"Nothing." I didn't meet his eyes as I came up with

a lie. "For a moment there, I thought I remembered something."

"If you want to ride Saturn, it'll have to be in a few days. I want to give him a chance to get used to his surroundings. Then you can give him a try."

"Thanks." I was ridiculously pleased that he'd agreed to let me ride the horse.

"Sloan."

We turned to see Beatrice hurrying down the terrace steps. She was back in light-colored trousers and a shirt that flowed around her as she moved. "James wants to see you. He saw you riding this way from his window and sent me down to fetch you."

There was an urgency in her voice that caused me to ask, "Is something wrong?" I recalled how tired he'd looked when I'd left his room the night before."

Beatrice turned to me. "He had a restless night. He always does when he overexerts and goes off of his diet."

Her voice was mild and there was nothing in her tone or her eyes to indicate that she was accusing me. Still, I felt the tug of guilt.

"He'll be fine. He's calling me up there to yell at me over something or other." Sloan tied Saturn to a post on the balustrade of the terrace. At Beatrice's pointed look, he pulled his cell phone out of his pocket. "I'll have one of the stable hands come up and fetch him."

Then in a quick movement that took me by surprise, he cupped the back of my neck with his free hand and lowered his mouth to mine. The contact was brief, hard and possessive, and it was enough to bring back all the sensations of both kisses we'd shared the day before. My insides heated and began to melt. I wasn't even aware I'd grabbed handfuls of his shirt until he drew away.

I had enough wits left to recognize satisfaction on his face before he said, "I'll pick you up at ten for the tour."

As he strode up the steps and disappeared into the house, I found myself both envious and a bit annoyed that he could walk. I wasn't at all certain that I could.

Something drew my eyes to one of the balconies that graced the second- and third-story bedrooms, and I saw that Austin was standing almost directly overhead. Our gazes held for a moment and I thought I saw a look of pure hatred before he turned abruptly and disappeared into his room. I couldn't help wondering if Sloan had known he was there when he kissed me.

"I thought you might like me to show you around the house so that you'll be familiar with it," Beatrice said.

I turned to find that she was regarding me with the most intent expression I'd yet seen on her face. "I'd like that very much. If you're sure you have the time."

"I'll make the time. I enjoy showing off the hacienda." She glanced down at the slim gold watch on her wrist and when her gaze returned to mine, her eyes were once more unreadable. "I have something to attend to in the greenhouse, but it should only take me twenty minutes or so."

"I'll meet you here."

Without another word, she turned and walked away down the path.

"Breakfast is about to be served," Marcie called from the terrace doors.

As I joined her, I wondered if she, too, had seen Sloan kiss me. Had he done it for our multiple audiences? And I couldn't help but wonder if that was the way he'd kissed my sister. More guilt tugged at me. I was sinking deeper and deeper and I was beginning to wonder how in the world I was going to get out.

"This has got to be difficult for you," Marcie said as we sat down at the table. "Not remembering anything."

Understatement of the year was my first thought. "Yes, it is. Would you mind telling me how I came to hire you?"

If the question surprised her, she covered beautifully. "I met you at a fund-raiser about six months ago. I was working for the woman who was cochair of the event. You mentioned to her that you were looking for an assistant, so I sent you a résumé. We met for lunch—I guess it was my interview, because you hired me over dessert."

"And what is it I hired you to do?" I asked.

She smiled. "I'm supposed to keep you organized. I also handle correspondence, keep track of your calendar and generally serve as your gal Friday."

"Are you good at it?"

She met my gaze steadily. "Yes, I am."

I really wanted to believe her. After all, my sister had hired her. And if I hadn't known about her brother's connection to those land developers, I might have.

She picked up her mug, then set it down. "I know that you have a crowded schedule today, so I'll get right to the point. I want to apologize for Austin's behavior last night." Marcie ran her finger around the rim of her mug. "You have no way of knowing this, but he's not usually like that."

"You mean he's not usually rude?"

"No." The corners of her mouth lifted in a wry smile. "He can be extremely charming when he wants to. But he's different when he drinks. He doesn't usually drink that much," she hurried to assure me. "Well, not anymore. He used to. But he's changed. This is difficult to explain. Your father has never given him the kind of responsibility that Austin wanted and thought he deserved. When Sloan left five years ago, Austin thought that at last James would turn to him, but instead, he started giving more responsibility to you. These last few weeks while you've been away, his uncle has finally given him the chance to prove his worth to McKenzie Enterprises. And he's done well. The surprise of seeing you last night made him think it would all slip away from him again. He's very embarrassed about his behavior."

I was pleased when Elena appeared with our breakfasts because I wasn't sure how to reply to what Marcie had said. It certainly confirmed what I'd been thinking the night before. Austin wasn't happy to have me back at the hacienda, and he could have been the one to rifle through my bag. He could have discovered my cell phone number simply by turning it off and then turning it on again, then made the threatening call later.

And if he was truly as sorry for his behavior as Marcie was professing, why wasn't he here in person to make his apology?

Marcie waited until Elena had returned to the kitchen before she said as if she'd read my mind, "Austin would be here himself, but he has a bit of a hangover."

I avoided making a comment by sampling the eggs and I immediately envied my sister for having a cook like Elena. Back in L.A., breakfast was something I ate on the fly—a granola bar if I'd remembered to grocery shop or a muffin out of a vending machine at work. With coffee—lots of it. I took another sip from my mug, trying to decide how to frame the question. Finally, I asked, "Why is it that my father waited until I disappeared to give Austin the kind of job he wants?"

Marcie set her fork down. "Austin has never been able to compete with you or Sloan. He doesn't have a natural love of horses the way that you and Sloan do. In college, he decided to rebel and he picked up the reputation of being a bit of a playboy. But that's not who he is, not really. And he's really good at the PR end of the business. I'm hoping that you'll give him a chance to continue to prove that. He'll be an asset to McKenzie Enterprises."

"Unless he's drinking too much to keep his mind on business," I said.

She leaned toward me. "He won't. If you'll just give him a chance to prove himself. That's one of the reasons I asked you to come riding with us this afternoon. I hope that Austin's behavior last night won't make you change your mind. It will give you a chance to get to know him a little better. And we can show you the ranch."

The idea of being alone and away from the ranch with two people who had motive and opportunity to search my duffel and make the threatening phone call I'd received should have made me wary.

But Marcie looked so sincere, so desperate, and I had to add in the fact that Cameron must have trusted her. But what finally decided me was that my inner Alice wanted to know more about both of them. "Of course, I'll go with you. How about we meet at the stables at three o'clock?"

"Thank you." She reached out and took my hand. "Thank you so much."

Her relief was palpable, and I suddenly realized that Marcie Linton was either in love with Austin or she was a good enough actress to audition for a part on *Secrets*.

11

"THIS IS THE BALLROOM." Beatrice led the way into one more cavernous room. The walls were a rich ochre color, and the deep red velvet drapes were pulled back from the floor-to-ceiling windows. Five crystal chandeliers, even larger than the ones in the dining room, hung from the ceiling. There were two large fireplaces, one at either end of the room, and the honey-colored oak floors were unmarred by carpets.

"Lovely," I murmured. It was a word that I'd repeated often during my tour. As I'd followed Beatrice down long hallways and through a myriad of salons, parlors and bedroom suites, I couldn't help but imagine what it must have been like growing up in a place like this. Hide-and-seek games could have gone on forever. And Cameron would have had two siblings to play with—Austin and Sloan. So far my absolute favorite space had been the library with its floor-to-ceiling shelves filled with books. One wall, nearly all glass, had let the garden in. To me it was paradise. I could have lingered there all day, but Beatrice allowed no loitering. She was on a schedule. She reminded me a lot of my resident advisor in college, the one Pepper and I had "borrowed" a car from. I wondered not for the first time how she and

James could be brother and sister. He was so outgoing, and she was so contained.

"Countess Montega had her wedding celebration here, and since then it's been a tradition that all the hacienda's brides hold their receptions here. Except for you." The tone held just a hint of censure. "Because of the small group of people who will be there, your father wants to use the parlor and the dining room. We'll have dancing on the terrace."

Feeling guilty, I said, "I'm sorry that Dad is rushing this wedding. It's got to be a lot of work for you, but I couldn't talk him out of it."

Her brows shot up. "From the time you were born, you've always been able to wrap your father around your little finger."

"Not about this. I couldn't. I thought that I might be able to reason with him last night after everyone had left, but he looked so frail. I didn't have the heart."

I thought I saw a flicker of surprise in her eyes.

"If he would just wait, we could keep the tradition intact." She sighed. "But I couldn't talk him out of it, either."

I wondered if that's what she'd been doing in his bedroom this morning before she came to fetch Sloan. As we walked along, I asked, "What can I do to help?"

She turned in surprise. "Why nothing. You've always allowed me to make those kinds of decisions, said you were too busy to run the house. Are you going to want to change that arrangement after your wedding?"

"No. No, of course not."

Without further comment, Beatrice gestured toward the wall to our right. "The portraits of all the hacienda's brides are on the walls. This first one is of the Countess Montega."

What I saw was a small, dark-haired woman with very sad eyes. For some reason, my heart went out to her. "She looks so unhappy."

"She was," Beatrice said. "There are copies of her diaries in the library. It was an arranged marriage, and she was ill on the voyage over here. According to the story that's been handed down, Don Roberto Montega was anxious to have an heir, and she was able to produce one within the first year, but she never recovered her health. His second wife lasted longer—five years." She pointed to another portrait of a tall, more amply proportioned woman. "She gave him three more sons before she died of a fever."

There were two other Montega brides, all in black, neither of them smiling. According to Beatrice, they'd both died young, too.

A chill moved through me as I studied the portrait of the woman Beatrice had pointed out as the last of the Montega brides. I'd read about them when I'd done my research on the hacienda, but it was different standing there and seeing how young they really were. "The mistresses of this house don't seem to have very good luck."

Beatrice gestured to the next portrait. "This one did."

It was a picture of a laughing green-eyed woman with red hair. The emerald-green dress dipped low in the front and the skirt fell in overlapping ruffles to the floor. She was a bright relief after her more somberly dressed predecessors. "Who is this one?"

"That is my great-great-grandmother. The story goes

that Silas McKenzie rescued her out of a brothel and made her his bride."

I grinned, thoroughly intrigued. This was a piece of information that neither Pepper nor I had come across. "It sounds very romantic."

"To some it might sound that way."

I got the distinct impression that Beatrice wasn't among them. I wondered how I might work it into a story line. "I understand that Silas was a bit of a rogue himself."

For the first time, I saw just the hint of a smile curve Beatrice's lips. "True. I suppose you might say that they were well suited. And she *was* a fine gardener."

Ah, a saving grace, I thought.

"She produced three sons before she died. The hacienda brides usually have a knack for producing heirs."

And for dying young.

"Except for your father's brides," Beatrice said as she led the way to the next picture. "Neither of them gave him a son."

I glanced up to see a painting of a fragile-looking beauty with long blond hair and blue eyes. She wore a long-sleeved dress that matched the color of her eyes, and the cat on her lap was either Hannibal or one of his more recent ancestors.

"That's Sarah McKenzie."

Once again I marveled at how little in the way of feelings Beatrice allowed into her voice. This was the woman who'd deserted Beatrice's brother for Sloan's father. I stepped forward to study the portrait more closely. She was lovely with a kind of ethereal beauty that men might easily covet. "It must have been very hard for Dad when she ran away with Sloan's father."

Once again Beatrice's gaze grew intent. "How did you know that, or are you beginning to remember?"

"Sloan told me the story," I explained. Thank heaven he had. I was going to have to be careful to remember what I'd been told since my arrival and what I knew from Pepper's report.

"It was a scandal at the time. A McKenzie running away with a stable manager."

I heard just a hint of distaste in her voice.

"I imagine it must have been a blow to Dad both in a business and personal sense, losing both a stable manager and a wife."

"The business never faltered. My husband took over as manager of the stables. And James is very resilient. He married again in less than two years."

This time I was almost sure that I heard a note of disapproval in her voice. She led the way to the next portrait. "This is Elizabeth, your mother."

I simply stared at the portrait. I couldn't even put a word to what I was feeling. All I could think of was that the woman staring down at me could have been my sister. My heart had leaped to my throat and it beat there, fast and hard. Many of Elizabeth McKenzie's features were ones I saw in the mirror every day—the nose, the pointed chin, even the shape of the eyes. Hers were a darker shade and more hazel than green. Her hair was different, too, a dark blond, and she wore it in a long braid that fell over her shoulder.

Questions flooded my mind. Could this be my biological mother? How else could Cameron and I look so much like her? But if that were true, how could Cameron and I have been put up for adoption? Pepper had found adoption records for both of us. And someone else knew about those papers—the someone who'd sent me that anonymous letter.

Questions—too many of them were swirling around in my mind. And as usual, I was jumping to too many conclusions. I struggled to rein my imagination in.

"Do you remember her?"

Beatrice's calm voice helped me to get a grip. I couldn't ask any of my questions right now. Not until I knew more. Not until I figured out what had happened to make Cameron run away.

I turned to her. "No. I can see the resemblance, and I know that she must be my mother. But I don't remember her at all. How did she die? You never got to tell me last night."

"Come," Beatrice said. "I'll show you."

She led the way out of the ballroom and down the corridor to a wide oak door. "Your father keeps it locked," she explained as she drew an iron key out of her pocket and inserted it into the lock. "No one is supposed to come up here, but I do every once in a while. I used to love this place as a girl."

The door creaked on its hinges and Beatrice had to put her back into it to get it open. In front of us was a wooden staircase that curved upward hugging the stone wall and hanging next to us was a thick rope. With a sinking stomach, I realized that we were going to climb into the bell tower.

I didn't like heights. Two or three storeys—like the balcony in Cameron's room—was fine. But put me on a terrace or a balcony or, heaven forbid, a rooftop that was more than four or five stories above terra firma, and

I froze. My parents took me to Europe when I was fourteen, and I couldn't even kiss the Blarney Stone. I'd nearly had a panic attack when we went to the top of the Eiffel Tower.

I told myself that the bell tower was only five stories as we rounded the first curve and continued upward. The stairs were flanked by the stone wall on one side and a railing on the other. Following Beatrice, I stayed near the wall and kept my hand on it for support. My palms were slick with sweat. My breath was coming shorter now, and it didn't have anything to do with the fact that I was climbing stairs.

We reached the tower room much too quickly for my liking. It was small, not more than eight feet square. The bell was overhead, and the walls on each side were only waist high. Beatrice crossed to the wall that overlooked the front of the hacienda. "Isn't the view beautiful?"

"Yes." I was sure it was, but my eyes were shut. I couldn't bring myself to look yet. A cold sweat had formed on my forehead. Taking a deep breath, I placed my hand on the iron railing that ran along the top of the wall on all sides. Opening my eyes, I kept them downcast as I felt my way along. Then I raised my gaze to the bluffs that I'd stood on only yesterday. Of course, there I'd been careful to stay back from the edge. I'd be all right as long as I didn't glance down, I told myself.

Out of the corner of my eye, I could see the riding ring where Sloan was working Saturn. Knowing that he was there steadied me a bit.

"I've missed the bells," Beatrice said. "When I was a girl, they were rung for the Angelus at 6:00 a.m. and 6:00 p.m. every day."

"Is the bell broken?" I asked. I wasn't looking at the bluffs anymore, but at Sloan and the horse.

"No. But the tower has a bad history, I'm afraid. The first Countess Montega threw herself from this very spot."

My vision blurred, and I blinked my eyes to clear it.

"After her son was born, she fell into a habit of walking in her sleep. The official story goes that she wandered up here one night and fell."

I couldn't keep myself from picturing it in my mind—that tiny woman I'd seen in the portrait, climbing the stairs in her sleep, walking out into the tower and falling...falling....

A wave of dizziness moved through me. I gripped the railing with both hands now, and my vision blurred again. I could imagine how easily someone could fall over it.

"Of course, that was the story that they gave the priest," Beatrice continued. "If she'd committed suicide, she couldn't have been buried in the church. Her husband and son would never have been able to eventually rest beside her."

"You think she committed suicide?" I asked. I made the mistake of shifting my gaze to her, and another wave of dizziness washed over me.

"You saw her portrait—those sad eyes. I've read some of the entries in her diary. I think she was homesick for Spain, and I think she was unhappy in her marriage. One night she wandered up here, and it would be so easy to just lean over the edge and let yourself fall. Don't you think?"

I didn't want to think about it. I shifted my gaze back to Sloan and drew in a deep breath.

"Then everything would be all right," Beatrice continued. "The loneliness and pain would be ended."

Her tone was matter-of-fact, but her words effectively formed the image in my mind again. I took several quick steps back from the wall.

Beatrice reached out and grabbed my hand. The strength of her grip surprised me. "Be careful. The back wall is just behind you."

I turned to see that I was only a foot away from it. My head was spinning fast now. "I...I need to get out of here."

"Heights bother you? I had no idea," Beatrice said as she led me to the stairs.

"Yes." I slapped my hand against the stone wall to steady myself.

"Sit down," Beatrice instructed, "and put your head between your knees."

I did as she said, and after a moment the dizzy feeling subsided. When I raised my head, I found she was sitting next to me.

"I didn't realize you were afraid of heights. If I'd realized it, I wouldn't have brought you up here."

She sounded worried and sincere. It was the most emotion I'd ever heard in her voice. "I thought that if I brought you here, you might remember something."

"What would I remember? You said that the tower has been closed off for almost twenty-five years. So I could never have been up here before."

Beatrice's gaze became intent again as she studied me. "I thought you might recall the story. Your mother followed in the first bride, the Contessa's footsteps. She threw herself off of the tower. That's why your father locked the doors and forbade the ringing of the bells."

My mind filled again with the horrible image of someone falling to the ground below. My voice sounded hoarse to me when I said, "How old was I?"

"Just a baby." She laid her hand over mine, and without thinking, I gripped hers tightly.

For a moment, I concentrated on gathering myself. It wasn't just the vertigo that was affecting me. I was still struggling to absorb the suspicion that had formed in my mind when I'd looked at Elizabeth McKenzie's portrait—that I might be her biological daughter. I had to moisten my lips to ask, "Could you please tell me what you know?"

"It happened a few months after your father and mother brought you back from Europe," Beatrice replied.

"Why?"

"Why did she do it?" Beatrice's tone was musing now. "I don't suppose we'll ever know for sure. Doc Carter might give you more of an insight. Elizabeth never quite recovered from her pregnancy with you. She didn't want to have children. She had her art. She told me once that she hadn't even wanted a husband, but she'd fallen in love with James. And my brother can be very persuasive."

Tell me about it, I thought. Beatrice wasn't looking at me. She was looking straight ahead at the stone walls of the tower as she continued, "She agreed to have a child for James, and he's always blamed himself for her death."

I thought of how the story paralleled in a way my own adoption. My mother hadn't wanted to take a break from her medical training to carry a child. "Why didn't they just adopt?"

The look Beatrice gave me suggested that the answer

was obvious. "Your father wanted an heir, someone with McKenzie blood." Then she slipped her hand from mine, glanced down at her watch, and rose. "It's nearly nine-thirty. You'll want to change for your tour with Sloan."

I looked at my jeans. My elegant sister would probably not wear these even to ride around the ranch.

"We'll go down slowly. I'll lead the way, and you stay right behind me. If you get dizzy, we'll sit and rest."

As we descended the stairs, my mind continued to spin. But this time it was with questions. My inner Alice was now on full alert.

What had caused Elizabeth to commit suicide? And could her tragedy somehow be connected to her daughter's disappearance?

12

THE MOMENT I ENTERED my room, I raced for my cell phone to see if Pepper had called back. But I hadn't taken it with me—I'd barely wanted to touch it since that threatening call had come in last night. I hadn't recharged it, either, so I held my breath as I checked to see if the battery had worn down. It hadn't.

I sank onto the bed, and Hannibal voiced his disapproval. I turned to find him still on his self-claimed throne. He really gave added meaning to the phrase "squatter's rights."

"Don't you have to eat or pee or something?"

His only reply was a bland and superior stare. And no wonder. Of course, he didn't have to go anywhere to eat when I was providing a seemingly endless supply of cat tidbits. I rose and got him a few more from the cabinet. And I bet he had his own secret methods for exiting and entering Cameron's room when I wasn't there. He hadn't moved from his position during the night—not even when I'd climbed in and stolen one of the pillows for myself.

"Look," I said as he disposed of the cat treats. "I know this is hard for you. But we have a common goal. You want Cameron back and so do I. You might think about cooperating a bit."

He seemed to be listening; at least he wasn't licking his claws or hissing or making any other threatening gesture. Satisfied for the moment, I turned my attention back to the phone and saw the message light blinking. I held my breath while I retrieved it, but it was Pepper's voice with one word. "Call."

I punched her number into my phone, then held my breath again and prayed that she'd pick up.

She did on the second ring. "Brooke?"

"Yes."

"I've got an update. It looks like Austin and both Lintons were indeed in Las Vegas. At least, their credit cards were. Cole is checking it out further as we speak."

"Marcie Linton told me that Austin had reformed."

"As of five weeks ago, he hadn't. He dropped close to ten thousand as far as Cole can tell. Tomorrow, Cole's going to San Diego to check on the flower show that Beatrice was presenting at. Are you all right?"

"I'm fine." I'd had a little argument with myself about just how much I was going to tell her and I'd decided on as little as possible—and certainly not about the phone call. I didn't want her rushing out here with Cole. Not yet anyway. "But I think I may know who my mother is."

There was a beat of silence on the other end of the line. "Wait."

I could picture her grabbing her notebook, then turning to a fresh page.

"Okay, who?"

"Elizabeth McKenzie."

"James's second wife?" Pepper asked. I heard a little plop. Had she dropped her pencil?

"It shocked me, too. And I could be wrong. But I've seen her portrait and I look like her. The story they're telling here is that Cameron was born in Switzerland. I thought at first the trip might have been made to hide the fact that Cameron was adopted. But since I saw Elizabeth's portrait, I think the trip to Switzerland was for something else."

"To cover up that two little girls were born and only one was brought home?"

"Maybe." My stomach clenched. I was finding it hard to accept the fact that we were talking about me. The little girl that wasn't brought home.

"But why?" Pepper's tone was thoughtful and I could hear the tapping of a pencil. "I found adoption papers for both you and Cameron in the records of a private adoption agency here in the States and no clue as to the mother."

"Which effectively stopped you from checking further," I pointed out.

"Yes, it did."

I heard a trace of annoyance in her voice.

"A Doctor Carter went on the trip with James and Elizabeth."

"Hmmmmm," Pepper said. "I'll bet the good doctor is in this up to his ears."

"That would be my guess. He's a close family friend who appears to be very kind and concerned. I can't imagine him having anything to do with Cameron's disappearance, but I'm thinking he might have sent me the letter. And he doesn't have an alibi for the day of Cameron's disappearance. He claims he was home using this putting green he has in his backyard."

"I'll get my brother Luke to let his fingers do the

walking on his computer keyboard. He'll check out your good doctor and if there are any records anywhere, he's the best bet we have of getting to them."

Just talking to Pepper was settling my nerves a bit. There were answers to the questions that were whirling in my mind, and we'd get them.

"I'm liking less and less the fact that you're there alone," Pepper said. "Why don't I join you? You can say that you need the comfort of having a friend from your present close at hand while you're exploring your past. Something like that."

"No." I'd anticipated that Pepper would suggest something like this, so I was prepared. "I need you to find out more information for me. See what else you can find on Hal Linton, too. He made a move on me last night."

"Really?"

"I'd like to know what his relationship with Cameron was before she disappeared. In your report, you said they met through Austin and Marcie. If they were having an affair, someone in Linton's business circle might have been aware of it."

"I'm on it. Anything else?"

On impulse, I said, "Check into Beatrice's husband. He ran the ranch for a while after Sloan's father ran away with Sarah McKenzie. But he's not here anymore, and no one talks about him. I don't even know his first name."

"I'll get it." I could hear Pepper scribbling. "Cole thinks I made a mistake, that I should have talked you out of this masquerade—which is a dangerous plan. His words."

I drew in a deep breath. "Well, the good news is I'm going to be leaving here by Friday evening."

"That is good news," Pepper agreed. Then after a beat, she said, the frown clear in her tone. "That's tomorrow. It's not that I'm not happy about it, but why do you have to get out of there so soon?"

I cleared my throat. "Because James has decided to move up the wedding. Tomorrow night Sloan and Cameron are going to be tying the knot in a small, private ceremony in the hacienda's chapel."

"Wait. Time-out. He wants you to marry Sloan Campbell tomorrow?"

"That's right. But don't worry. That's not going to happen."

"Liar."

"I'm not kidding."

"I know you, Brooke. If you haven't found what happened to your sister by tomorrow, you won't leave."

"That's why I'm calling you. I need anything you can find out ASAP."

"I don't like this."

"Gotta go. Sloan is giving me a tour of the ranch to see if he can stir up any memories. Find out what you can."

"Brooke—"

"I'll check in with you later today so that you'll know I'm all right. Bye." I disconnected the call and frowned. She'd worry about me now. I couldn't help that. I was worried myself. But at least Pepper didn't know about the threatening phone call. And after a morning with Marcie and Beatrice, I wasn't one step closer to finding out who'd made it.

"Hey, Red?"

It was Sloan's voice. I hurried to the window and saw him standing in the garden below me. Once again, I felt a rush of pleasure just seeing him. Not good, I thought.

"Beatrice told me you were in your room. I'm running a little late, and I have to stop at the stables."

I glanced at my watch. "You said ten. I still have to change my clothes."

"When you're changed, come over to the carriage house. It'll save us some time."

"Sure."

With a little salute, Sloan turned and walked away. I kept my eyes on him as he strode down the same path he'd ridden on earlier with Saturn. He didn't look as though he was hurrying, but those long legs of his really ate up the ground.

And he belonged to my sister. I should write that on the palm of my hand the way I used to write reminders when I was in junior high.

The brush of something against my leg made me jump. Glancing down, I saw that it was Hannibal, and my heart returned to its usual place in my body. The cat flicked me a look and then rubbed against me again.

"Are you trying to suggest a truce, or are you warning me off Cameron's fiancé?"

Hannibal made a soft purring sound in his throat that I wasn't quite able to interpret. "I was just lecturing myself about the same thing. I'm going to have a talk with Sloan while we're taking our tour." And I was also going to find out why he hadn't tried to talk James out of moving the wedding up.

I'd tell him that I didn't want him to kiss me again. Which was a big fat lie. And he'd know it because so far my response to his kisses on a scale of one to ten could be measured at about a thirty.

Hannibal purred again. Did I actually hear a note of skepticism, or was I just projecting?

"I'll explain that I need time to get used to him again." Hopefully, that would work. But my eyes shifted back to Sloan. Who was I kidding? If I got any more used to him, I'd be in his bed. One more day, I reminded myself. Surely, I could keep from jumping his bones for that long.

"It isn't as though I don't have other things to occupy my time." Like finding out what had happened to my sister. And getting to the bottom of why I looked so much like Elizabeth McKenzie. I glanced at my cell phone. Not to mention, avoiding the fate of the previous mistresses of the Hacienda Montega.

"My plate's full," I assured Hannibal. And myself.

After taking one last look at Sloan, I turned and strode into the closet. Out of the corner of my eye, I saw Hannibal leap onto the bed, but he didn't go back to stake his claim on the pillows. Instead, he made a circle, then sat near the side where he could watch me select an outfit to wear.

Quickly, I located a pair of riding breeches and boots, but I couldn't decide on a blouse. Cameron seemed to have a weakness for silk, and I was torn between the peach, ivory or pale blue one. I held each in front of me. Hannibal growled at the blue one.

As I stripped off my jeans and T-shirt and dressed in Cameron's clothes, I couldn't help smiling at the idea that I was taking fashion advice from a cat. I wondered if this was something that he and Cameron did on a daily basis. I wanted to think that it was, that there was a softer side to the picture of my sister that everyone else was painting.

When I was done, I turned in a full circle for Hannibal's benefit. He made no further noise, nor did he make any threatening gestures. I decided to take his lack of reaction for approval, and I felt a little closer to my sister as I left the room.

THE CARRIAGE HOUSE had been built of the same colored stone as the hacienda, making me assume that it dated back to the same era. At one time, it had been used to store horse-drawn carriages. The lower floor had been renovated and now offered the modern convenience of automatic sliding doors.

It seemed a little far from the main house to use as a garage. Curious, I peeked through one of the glass windows and discovered there were indeed cars inside. The rugged truck that I'd seen Sloan use the day before along with its trailer, a black SUV with the logo of the ranch on it, and a sporty little red convertible that only seated two. It was built for speed, and it was exactly the kind of car that I hoped to own one day.

Was it Sloan's? Or perhaps it was Cameron's.

At the side of the building, I found a set of iron stairs to the second floor. On my way up I reviewed in my mind what I was going to tell Sloan—that I needed time to get to know him better and it would be better if he didn't kiss me again.

That at least wasn't a lie. It would be a lie if I told him I didn't *want* him to kiss me again. I knocked on the screen door.

After waiting a bit, I knocked again. When there was

still no response, I allowed my inner Alice to open the door and walk into a spacious kitchen that was neat as a pin. Two arches in the wall to my right allowed access to other rooms. Through the far one came the sound of running water and a man singing.

I moved to the closest arch and spotted a large flat-screen TV, what looked to be a state-of-the-art CD player, and two large speakers. Boy toys. There was a comfortable-looking leather couch, and an oak coffee table with a paperback book lying open facedown to mark the page. There were more books in built-in glass-doored bookcases that flanked the fireplace.

My gaze shifted to the art on the walls, and moving closer, I saw that each piece held four photos that had been clustered in the center, then matted and framed. In one group, I saw a man who resembled Sloan standing next to a horse with a baby in his arms. The same man was captured in other poses, two with James. Sloan's father?

In another, there was a cluster with James and an older boy. He looked to be five or six in one, a teenager in another, and in the others he was a man—Sloan Campbell. It was like having a family album on the walls. Except there were two families and the mother was missing in each set of photos.

Cameron and he had that in common—a mother they'd never known. In spite of that loss, I envied Sloan in a way. My own family was not the type to take photos. There were no albums, no framed pictures on the walls. The ones I had were some that friends like Pepper had snapped and given to me. I glanced around the room and realized that there were no pictures of Cameron—not as a little girl and not as a woman. I found that odd.

Slowly but surely, I was learning about Sloan Campbell. He was a man who worked hard, was good at what he did, and who liked a comfortable, quiet place to come home to at night. I suppose that didn't make him much different from a lot of men. Or women. I liked to come home to a quiet space myself.

My sister, on the other hand, evidently liked to go out, to meet clients for dinner and drinks—if I could make judgments by her wardrobe and what others had told me.

The singing had stopped, but I could still hear water running as I returned to the kitchen. I knew I was pushing it but I quietly opened the two cupboards that framed the sink. Dishes were stacked in neat piles, mugs arranged in rows. One drawer contained towels, the other a minimal selection of flatware. Then I just had to open Sloan's refrigerator. You could tell a lot from a person's refrigerator. I'd once had Mallory Carstairs take an inventory of the contents of her current lover's fridge and decide to break off the affair. He had been planning to kill her and the telltale mushrooms were right there on the bottom shelf.

There were no mushrooms in Sloan's fridge. In fact there wasn't much in the way of food at all. He kept it stocked with bottled water and beer. The top shelf held a bottle of white wine—the same Chardonnay that he'd claimed was Cameron's favorite. Behind it was a paper bag. Opening it, I saw it contained cheese—three kinds—and a bag of plump green grapes.

"Hungry, Red?"

I dropped the bag and whirled around to face Sloan. "I—"

For the life of me I couldn't get another word out. He

was standing in the archway wearing only a pair of jeans, bare-chested and barefoot. I could see that his skin was still a bit damp from his shower. Heat flooded through me. I tried to tell myself that it was from embarrassment because he'd caught me snooping, but that was a lie. It was Sloan who was making my body burn and my mouth water. Oh, I was hungry all right. Only it wasn't for food. I wanted a taste of Sloan Campbell.

13

"HUNGRY, RED?" He definitely was, Sloan thought as she jumped and whirled to face him. He'd been watching her for some time as she'd poked through his cupboards and studied the contents of his refrigerator as if there was some secret there she was determined to discover. Her concentration had been total. He'd seen the same intentness the evening before when he'd been introducing her to family and guests, and he couldn't help wondering if she would bring that same concentration to the task of making love to a man. To him.

He'd spent a sleepless night trying to talk himself out of what he was going to do. He'd even tried to sell himself on the idea that if he could have her just once, he could get her out of his system. He hadn't been successful at either endeavor.

He wanted her. She wanted him. That was the one truth between them. He was going to start there, and see where it would lead. And for the first time in his life Sloan was going to damn the consequences. But he'd wanted to choose the time and the place. And he had. He'd chosen the perfect spot, and he'd planned to take her there.

He studied her now as she stood silently regarding him. She was wearing Cameron's clothes, well-tailored

riding breeches and one of the silk blouses Cameron
always favored. He even caught a hint of the scent that
Cameron always wore. But it wasn't Cameron's eyes he
was looking into. Her eyes had never held that combi-
nation of heat and promise and innocence. He wasn't
sure which pulled at him more or which caused the
desire building inside of him to turn so quickly into a
burning ache.

What he was sure of was that his plans had changed.
The time and the place was now.

"I thought we'd take the wine and grapes with us,"
Sloan said as he walked toward her. "There's a place I'm
going to show you, your favorite place on the ranch, and
I thought we'd have a picnic. But we could enjoy them
now. If you think you can't wait."

"WAIT..." My voice was working. Now all I needed was
some more words. Thoughts would be good, too. They'd
drained out of my mind the moment I saw him standing
there. Now that he'd moved closer, I could feel his heat
and the sensation was only heightened by the coolness
of the open refrigerator at my back. I felt trapped
between ice and fire. I took a breath and drew in his
scent—soap and something uniquely male, something
that was Sloan Campbell. It made my mouth water.

I had to say something. Anything. "I...was
just...snooping. I'm sorry. I once read that you can learn
a lot about a person from what he or she keeps in their
refrigerator. And so I thought I would take a look
and—" Now I was babbling. I bit down on my lip
because if I kept it up, I might give myself away.

"What did you learn about me?" He took a step closer.

"I…" Just as quickly as it had come, the power to form words and string them into sentences deserted me again. When Sloan touched my arm, I jolted.

"Easy," he said in the same kind of tone I'd heard him use on Saturn. "I just want to shut the refrigerator door."

Keeping his hand on my arm, he picked up the bag, replaced it on the shelf and closed the door.

When he finally turned back to me, I found myself pinned against the counter.

"So what did you learn about me?"

I cleared my throat. "You don't cook much here."

"Thanks to Elena, I don't have to. She spoils me. Is that all you learned?"

"You like to read." I thought of the photos in the living room. "I think that family is important to you. I looked in the other room. I was curious, and when you didn't answer my knock, I just—"

"You don't have to apologize. Given the chance, I'd love to search the place where you've been staying for the last five weeks. I'm curious about you, too."

It was a mistake to keep looking into his eyes. The heat there was even more intense than what I was already feeling. He rubbed his thumb over my bottom lip, and I heard my breath catch.

"You're so responsive." He lifted his other hand to cup the back of my neck.

I knew what Sloan was going to do. He was going to kiss me. So I raised a hand and pressed it against his chest. Big mistake. His skin felt like warm velvet stretched over steel. The hand at my neck was hard, too. Heat rocketed through me from both contact points.

"I want to kiss you."

"No." I don't know how in the world I got the word out. It was such a lie that I marveled lightning didn't strike me dead. Never had my mind and body been so diametrically opposed.

"Why not?"

Desperately, I tried to remember my sister and what I'd come here to do. I moistened my lips. "That's what I came to talk to you about."

"About kissing?" He rubbed the pad of his thumb over my bottom lip again.

"No. About *not* kissing. I know that you probably were curious on the bluff and again last night in the garden, and then this morning you kissed me again to make a point to Marcie and Hal and Beatrice. I understand that. But I don't want you to kiss me anymore."

"Liar."

Okay. So I desperately wanted him to kiss me again. And wanted to kiss him back. And more.

"You're wrong about why I kissed you." His thumb began a gentle stroking up and down the back of my neck. Any minute I was going to evaporate into steam.

"Each time I kissed you it was because I wanted to. Because I couldn't help myself."

"Really?" He didn't look entirely happy about that. Still, at his admission, a mix of pleasure and astonishment flooded through me. The fact that he could be feeling the same kind of attraction, the same level of lust that I was feeling made my knees go even weaker.

"In a minute, if you don't let me go, I won't be able to help myself, either," I said.

"You can't say something like that to me and expect me not to act on it."

I could have moved then. I didn't.

He did. His mouth covered mine, and there was nothing of the gentle exploration that he'd used in the garden the night before. Today his lips were hard, his tongue and teeth demanding. Little explosions of pleasure shot through me, making my hunger build with a speed I'd never experienced before. My tongue met his, tangling and caressing. I tasted the hot, minty flavor of his toothpaste and something darker that reminded me of chocolate, only better.

When he bit my bottom lip, pleasure sharpened. I wrapped my arms around him, flattened my palms against that hard smooth skin and tried to absorb him. When hard hands cupped my bottom, I scooted up to wrap my legs around his hips. Through layers of clothes, I felt the rigid length of his penis pressed against my center, and I rubbed myself against it.

With a groan, he eased me onto the edge of the counter and broke off the kiss. For a moment, we were both oxygen starved and breathing hard. He drew away, just a little. But he didn't release me entirely. He left one hand on my side, his thumb stroking my nipple. The palm of his other hand lay heavily on my thigh, and that thumb was moving up and down between my legs, teasing, promising. The friction at both contact points had me quivering with need.

Sloan's eyes were narrowed, and his voice was husky when he spoke. "If you want me to stop, say so now."

He was giving me a choice. But with his hands on me, I couldn't seem to say a thing. All I wanted was him, hot and hard inside of me. I couldn't think of anything else.

"If you don't say something, I'm going to take it as a yes."

My inner Alice was shouting yes. My saner self, the part that always reminded me of the trouble I usually got into when I gave in to impulse, remained silent.

Still he hesitated as if he needed some sign from me. "Yes or no?"

This was wrong. It had to be. But I didn't care. I'd never felt this way before. Maybe I never would again. "Yes."

It was triumph now that I saw in his eyes. Then he lifted me off the counter and carried me through the archway and into the bedroom. He laid me on the bed, and then he positioned himself on top of me. My legs parted for him, and once he'd settled between them, he rocked against me. I arched up or tried to. But I was trapped beneath him. His legs were hard between mine, and I could feel the hardest part of him—a solid ridge of granite—pressing against me through way too many layers of clothes.

Then he levered himself off me, and settling himself beside me, he took my wrists in one hand and pinned them above my head.

I started to protest, but he countered by kissing me again. My head began to spin. He still held my hands above my head, and with his foot, he'd pinned one of my ankles to the bed. With his free hand he began to unbutton my blouse, slowly, tantalizingly. Each sensation was so intense—the heat of his body beside me, the dark, rich taste of him and the slow movement of those fingers as they released one button after another. Each time they slipped beneath the silk and brushed my skin I trembled. All the while he feasted on my mouth, exploring every part of it in slow strokes of his tongue as if there was some flavor there he hadn't yet sampled.

Sloan tugged the blouse free of my slacks and pushed it aside. Then he raised his head and looked down at what he'd uncovered. "Pretty," he murmured in a husky voice as he ran the palm of his hand over my breast. Through my thin bra of silk and lace, I felt the heat of his touch like a little electric shock. I did my best to arch into his palm.

"I've been wanting to touch you, really touch you." He paused to move his hand lower until it rested flat on my stomach. "Ever since you appeared out of nowhere on that bluff." He undid the button of my riding pants and drew the zipper down slowly. The sound it made as it opened was incredibly erotic.

"Your skin is so soft. Like rainwater." He pressed his hand against my stomach and lowering his head, he covered my breast with his mouth. Ever so slowly, he began to stroke my nipple with his tongue. The moist heat of his mouth combined with the friction of the silk against my skin had me trying to arch upward, reaching for more....

I whimpered something, and as if he had been waiting for that sound, he moved his hand lower on my stomach, sliding his fingers beneath my panties and then between my legs until he reached the spot that felt so empty. I stopped breathing then, trapped between exquisite pleasure and the painful ache that was building inside of me.

I tried to move and found that I was trapped physically, too. My hands were still pinned above my head, my foot still held captive by his. All I could manage to do was wiggle my hips, but it wasn't enough.

"Please." My voice was barely a thread of sound, and

just as I thought I might die of wanting, he drew my nipple into his mouth, sucking it hard at the same moment that he pushed two fingers into me.

"Sloan," I cried out.

He drew his fingers out and pushed them in, drew out, pushed in, matching the rhythm of his hand to the movement of his mouth as he suckled at my breast. I was burning, melting, searching....

And then suddenly he withdrew from me. The sense of loss was so acute that for a moment, I couldn't say anything. Even though he'd released my hands and my foot, I couldn't move. I watched him rise from the bed and begin to take off his jeans. My gaze followed the dark denim as it slid down those long muscled legs. Beneath them he wore white Jockey briefs, and I could see the evidence of his arousal pushing at the fabric. When the underwear followed the path of the jeans, I finally saw what I'd only felt before. My mouth went dry as dust. He was so big—not just where my eyes were currently glued, but all over. His chest was wide, the bronze skin sprinkled with dark hair, and he had the shoulders of a linebacker. I had never wanted anyone the way I wanted him.

"Hurry," I said. At least that's what I tried to say. The sound that came out was more like a moan.

And he didn't hurry at all. At least not to the bed. Instead, he moved to the bedside table, opened the drawer and took out a condom. I'd thought the sound of my zipper opening was erotic, but the rip of that foil packet topped it. When he'd fully sheathed himself, I sat up and said, "Hurry."

He didn't move. He simply stood there, looking

down at me. My skin had chilled when he'd moved away so abruptly, but now it began to heat again.

"You have too many clothes on," he said.

Glancing down, I realized that I was still mostly clothed. I'd been so mesmerized watching him strip that I'd completely forgotten.

"Take them off for me." His voice was husky, but I found the thread of command in his voice arousing. And he was driving me mad. He'd been teasing and tormenting me, taking me right to the brink and then withdrawing. Maybe it was time I gave as good as I was getting.

Raising my eyes to meet his, I deliberately started with my boots. I dropped one and then the other over the side of the bed. I took my socks off next, drawing out the process as long as I could. His eyes narrowed and I could hear the harsh sound of his breathing in the room. I turned my attention to my bra next. It was a good thing that he'd unbuttoned my blouse because my fingers were growing numb. Then lying back down, I lifted my hips off of the bed and began to wiggle out of my riding breeches.

I'd only managed to get them halfway down my legs when he joined me on the bed and dragged them off the rest of the way. Then Sloan knelt between my legs and tore away the lace that still separated us. Power streamed through me as he gripped my hips and positioned himself over me. But then once again, he paused.

I wrapped arms and legs around him. "Dammit, Sloan. Do it."

He framed my face with his hands. "Do what?"

"Come inside me. I want you inside right now."

He drove into me, and I went off like a rocket. The

orgasm ripped through me so fast and so hard that I think I lost consciousness for a moment. The next thing I knew, my arms had dropped away from him and so had my legs. They felt like limp noodles. But Sloan was still on top of me, still filling me.

I opened my eyes to find him regarding me in that intent way he had. I read triumph and satisfaction in his eyes. And something. A question?

He withdrew and pushed into me again. To my astonishment my knees came up and my arms wrapped themselves around him.

"Hold on," he said in a hoarse voice. "It's going to be a rough ride."

It was. And incredibly I was ready for it. As he drove into me again and again, each stroke built in speed and intensity. My world narrowed to this man, the heat and hardness of his body, his hands, and the movement of him inside of me. I felt another climax building, more slowly this time, but as we raced toward it together, I felt parts of myself slipping away.

"Come with me." His voice was harsh in my ear. "Now."

I had no choice. When the first wild spasm tore through me, I cried out. But it didn't end there. He showed me more, driving me up again until I knew only that searing heat. And him. His voice joined mine as I gave myself to him and we flew over that last peak together.

Sloan came back to awareness slowly. He couldn't think. All he knew were sensations. His face was buried in Red's hair, his body pressing hers into the mattress. His heart was racing, his breath coming in gasps.

And he was trembling. That was a first. A little sliver of fear moved through him. What in the world was she doing to him? Still dazed, he raised his head and studied her. Her eyes were half-closed, her skin still flushed from passion.

He'd wondered where it would lead when he made love to her. But he hadn't expected this...this loss of self. How could he? How could a man anticipate something he'd never experienced before? Something he was already wanting to experience again.

Incredibly, he felt a fresh wave of desire ripple through him. How could she do this to him—this woman who looked so much like Cameron. But who wasn't Cameron.

"Who the hell are you?"

14

"WHO THE HELL ARE YOU?"

The question, especially the not-so-friendly tone of it, blew some of the fuzz out of my brain. I opened my mouth, not at all sure what was going to come out, but Sloan pressed a finger against my lips to silence me.

"Don't even think of lying, Red. I know that you're not Cameron McKenzie."

Okay, the jig was up. There was always the possibility that someone would see through my impersonation. But I couldn't think of a worse spot to be in—lying naked beneath the man who'd just unmasked me. Worse than that, I was lying naked beneath a man I'd just had mind-blowing sex with. A man that I incredibly wanted again, so my brain was still deep in the fuzzy zone. Otherwise, I might have thought up something. Anything.

"What's your name?"

"Brooke Ashby."

"Brooke Ashby." He said the name as if he were testing it on his tongue. "I can check it out."

"Yes, you can." Temper began to flare inside of me. "And you can get off me."

He rubbed his thumbs over my cheekbones, and something else began to fire up inside of me.

"I'm not moving until you tell me what game you're playing, Brooke Ashby."

"Game?"

"You come here with an amnesia story and pass yourself off as Cameron McKenzie. Several scenarios have occurred to me. In one of them, I figure you came across a picture of Cameron, were struck by the resemblance, and decided that impersonating her was the ticket to getting your hands on her inheritance."

I stared at him. Had seducing me been just part of his plan to unmask me? Well, I didn't like his tactics. Or rather I'd liked them too much.

"Get off me!" I shoved hard against his shoulders, but I might as well have been trying to move one of those boulders on the bluff. "What kind of man are you? You thought that I would do something like that and…and yet you made love to me?"

"Yeah. And I want to again."

I felt the truth of what he was saying inside me. And I felt my body's reaction. There was a part of me that was angry, but there was also a part of me that was almost weeping to have him moving in me again. Since I wasn't having much luck controlling how my body was responding, I concentrated on keeping my brain unfuzzed. "That's not going to happen."

"Yeah, it is." As if to prove his point, he surged forward, and we both felt the way my body reacted. Heard the way my breath caught in my throat.

Sloan withdrew. "We'll get to that in a minute. First, I want the truth about what you're doing here."

"I'll need to breathe. And I'll be able to think more clearly if you get off of me."

"Fair enough." He rolled to my side, but he kept an arm around my waist and one leg over mine. "But you're not getting out of this bed until you answer my questions."

My mind raced for a moment trying to decide just what to tell him. But he hadn't moved far enough away for me to completely get the static out of my brain.

Finally, I did what I usually do when my back is against the wall. I went with impulse. Not that following my impulses always got me out of scrapes. Case in point—giving in to my impulse to make love with Sloan Campbell. But I wanted to tell someone, and since Sloan already knew that I was an imposter, he was the most likely candidate and perhaps he could be useful. "If I tell you, will you help me find out what happened to Cameron?"

His gaze remained steady on mine. "Then she didn't send you here?"

"No. Why would you think that? Oh. The face-saving thing again? She sends me here to seduce you. Then she has a good reason not to go through with the wedding." I stared at him. It would make a great story line for Mallory Carstairs on *Secrets*. But... "Would Cameron actually do something like that?"

"She has a lot of her father in her. She likes to play games."

Evidently, the big difference between Cameron and me was that I could dream up plot lines, but she could really carry them out.

"Did James have a hand in your coming here?" Sloan asked.

"No. And you haven't answered my question. If I

tell you, will you help me find out what's happened to Cameron?"

"Why do you think something's happened to her?"

"Because I'm her twin, and I can feel it."

Surprise flickered over his face. "Her twin?" He frowned. "I don't think so. Cameron doesn't have a twin sister."

"I didn't think I had one, either, until five weeks ago. That's when I received an anonymous letter telling me that I was adopted."

I found that telling him about the letter was like pulling my finger out of a dike. Everything else came pouring out with it. I told him about talking to my parents and how they'd confirmed I was adopted and that my whole life had been a lie. I told him about hiring Pepper and what she'd discovered and my decision to come to the ranch to find out what I could about Cameron.

Spilling all the beans probably wasn't my wisest strategy, but Sloan was a good listener. He didn't interrupt, didn't react in a judgmental way. And it was helping, I found, to put everything I'd discovered so far into words.

I also became aware that lying there in his bed and revealing all my secrets to him was almost as intimate as making love with him had been. For a while after I was finally finished, he didn't say a word. My insides twisted into knots. What must he think of me? I claimed that I'd come to the ranch to find out what had happened to my newly discovered sister, and as part of my little adventure, I'd agreed to marry him on Friday and then I'd slept with him. Looking at it from an objective point of view, his scenario about my coming here seemed a lot more feasible than the truth.

But when he finally spoke, all Sloan said was, "So you're telling me that you believe Cameron and you are twin sisters, separated at birth and both put up for adoption."

"Yes. Except Cameron wasn't adopted, was she?"

He was looking at me in that intent way he had. "No. At least not that I'm aware of."

"Beatrice gave me a tour of the ballroom this morning, and I saw Elizabeth McKenzie. I could be her daughter. Cameron and I could both be her daughters."

"You're implying that Elizabeth had twins and she and James gave one of you up? I can't see James doing that."

I was having trouble with that, too. "And it doesn't explain my friend Pepper's discovery of Cameron's adoption records. She's checking into it again. But that's not what's important right now. What's important is to find Cameron. I have a really bad feeling—I've had it ever since I found out that she was missing—that something bad has happened to her. She didn't just go off in a snit like everyone seems to think. What did the two of you argue about?"

"I caught her kissing Hal Linton in the garden. After I sent him off, I reminded her that part of our agreement was that although our marriage was partly a business arrangement, we would be monogamous. She lost her temper then. But I don't think what I said was the only thing that set her off. Something else was bothering her. Anyway, she said she was going to call off the wedding. And I told her to go ahead. I knew that once she thought it over, she'd back down. Cameron never accepts criticism well. When she went missing, none of us were worried about her. It's not unusual for her to disappear like that."

"But five weeks? You think she needs that much time to figure out whether or not she wants to go through with the wedding?"

"It's possible that she's decided to call it off. She doesn't like to back down once she's given her word. So she may be figuring out how to persuade her father to side with her on this."

He didn't sound angry or upset that Cameron might be deciding to call off the wedding. I tried not to read too much into that because whatever the truth was surrounding Cameron and Sloan's marriage, it didn't change the fact that I'd just made love with my sister's fiancé. Or the fact that I wanted to do it again. I was all too aware of the strength and the heat of his arm lying across my stomach.

As if he were reading my mind, Sloan slid his hand up to cup my breast, and my nipples—traitors that I'd already found them to be—hardened.

"Don't," I said. But my voice didn't sound convincing even to me. In spite of the satisfaction I'd experienced only a short time before, my body was already heating, yearning.

"Why not?"

I nearly cried out in protest when he removed his hand and levered himself into a sitting position.

"Because…"

My voice trailed off when I saw that instead of leaving, he was taking off the condom and replacing it with another.

I just lay there mesmerized, watching him do it. I couldn't think of my sister or the wedding or anything but making love to Sloan again. When I finally raised a hand, it wasn't to push him away. Oh no. Instead, I ran my fingers over the long hard length of him, and I wished I'd thought to do it before he'd slipped the latex on.

The sound he made deep in his throat echoed what I was feeling almost perfectly. He moved quickly then, first lifting away my hand and then finding a place for himself between my legs.

Exhibiting my usual total lack of control where he was concerned, I immediately wrapped arms and legs around him and arched upward.

But he didn't fill me. Instead, he said, "You haven't yet asked how I knew that you weren't Cameron."

I hadn't. It was a sure sign of how far gone I was that my inner Alice hadn't kicked in on that little issue. "How?"

He leaned down to brush his mouth over mine. "Your reaction to Saturn was a clue. At the Derby, Cameron was afraid of him. He didn't take to her, either." He paused to trail a line of kisses along my jaw.

When his teeth nipped my earlobe, pleasure fizzed through me. "But that wasn't it."

His voice was a husky whisper in my ear, and I could feel him against me right where I needed him. But it wasn't enough. He wasn't letting me move, and I wasn't sure I could speak.

"It was when I kissed you the first time on the bluff, I knew that you weren't Cameron, and in the garden last night, I confirmed it. You see, I never kissed Cameron quite that way before, and I never wanted to do this to her."

He entered me in one fast plunge, filling me so completely I cried out.

"I don't want to stop doing this to you, Brooke." He withdrew and pushed into me again. And again. True to his word, he didn't stop for a very long time.

WHEN I COULD FINALLY breathe and think again, I found that Sloan and I were lying side-by-side, tucked together like spoons, and as much as I knew I should, I didn't want to move. This was why forbidden fruit was forbidden, I reminded myself—the addiction factor.

"We'll have to tell James," Sloan finally said.

"No." I wiggled around to face him. "We can't. Not yet. If we do, I'll have to stop impersonating Cameron, and having amnesia gives me the perfect excuse to ask a lot of questions."

He studied me. "Questions about what?"

"About who was around on the day Cameron disappeared." I swallowed hard. "And about who might benefit if she doesn't come back."

"Because you have a 'feeling' she was the victim of foul play?"

He was frowning, and I could still hear skepticism in his tone. So I drew in a deep breath and told him about the anonymous phone call I'd received.

When I was finished, he continued to study me with that I-can-see-right-through-you look of his.

"Cameron is an heiress," I said. "You were quick enough to jump to the conclusion that I came here masquerading as her to get her money. What happens if she never comes back and your marriage can't take place? What will James do with the estate then?"

"I don't know. But I imagine he'll do a variation of what he intended to do before Cameron and I agreed to marry. In his current will he leaves Cameron the estate and the land, but all of the decisions about running the ranch and the business, including any sale of the land, is placed under the control of a board of directors, a group handpicked by James. He's been pretty close-mouthed about whom he's selected, but my guess is that Doc Carter would be on it, perhaps Rachel Lakewood and Jack Boland. They are all close friends of James and very like-minded. James would like to have control of this place even from the grave."

"But he was going to give that up and turn the place over to you and Cameron if you marry because…?"

Sloan gave me a wry smile. "My guess is that Cameron gave him an offer he couldn't refuse. She'd marry someone he'd approve of with the ability to run the ranch just as well as his hand-selected board, and he'd have at least the hope of grandchildren. That's just a guess on my part, but she'd know what kind of a carrot to dangle in front of her father. Of course, it could have been that the marriage part was James's idea. A carrot he dangled in front of Cameron's nose—marry someone I approve of and I'll leave you both everything."

"And Cameron chose you?"

"Perhaps. It could have been James's idea. He didn't want me to leave five years ago, and he knows how much I love this place. He also knew what to dangle in front of me to get me to come back."

I swallowed hard again. I didn't like putting my growing suspicion into words. "And if something has happened to Cameron, who would James leave the place to then? Beatrice and Austin with the board making all the decisions?"

"Probably. I hadn't given it any thought." His frown deepened. "But that would be a good guess, and I don't like where this is going."

"I don't, either. Who might know James's backup plan? Who would he confide in?"

"Doc Carter," Sloan said without hesitation. "He and James have been close since they were kids. James trusts him."

"Promise me you won't tell anyone yet who I really am, not until we know more about what might have happened to Cameron."

"And if something has happened to Cameron, your impersonation of her puts you in danger. I don't—"

I stopped him by putting my fingers against his lips. "Just until tomorrow. I'll have to let James know who I really am before the wedding."

For a moment, he hesitated. "On one condition."

"What?"

"We'll ask questions together. I don't want you wandering off with any of them alone. Whoever went through your things and left that message on your cell phone was at the hacienda last night."

"I agree and I promise."

He drew me into his arms and just held me. "Don't forget that there's at least one other person who hasn't been fooled by you."

"The person who sent me the anonymous letter." In spite of the warmth of Sloan's body, I felt a little chill move through me.

"Yeah," Sloan said. "Someone is playing a very deep game here. The question is who?"

SOON. SOON. SOON. The shadow waited in the shade of the trees, repeating the word over and over again until it became a chant. A promise. A prayer.

The mistakes of the past could be corrected. One could always achieve what one wanted with patience. And persistence. One didn't have to be second best. That perception could be corrected—with time.

She would be here very soon. She always came here. So predictable. That's what had made it so easy the last time.

And there would be no mistakes this time. Rage rose like a bitter-tasting bile and was quickly repressed. There was no need for anger or self-recrimination. Never again. Not when a mistake could be so easily remedied.

The shadow ran a hand over the weapon. The gun, a sleek Winchester, would ensure that this time the end would be final.

Soon.

15

"WE'RE TAKING A TOUR of the ranch in that?" I'd stopped short the moment I saw the shiny red plane on a short runway behind the stables.

"Yeah. Isn't she a honey?"

To me, the plane looked small, very small, like a shiny red kid's toy. And it had propellers. Sloan strode quickly toward it, and I had to double my pace to keep up. I glanced down at my breeches. "I thought we'd be riding."

Sloan climbed up on one of the wings, and held out a hand to me. "It's a big ranch, and believe me, this little beauty will be a lot easier on your seat than if we did the tour on horseback."

I let him help me up and I took a skeptical look into the tiny cockpit. "Where will the pilot sit?"

He laughed then. "I'm the pilot."

I turned to stare at him. "You fly?"

"James taught me when I was in my teens. Want to see my license?"

I could see the excitement in his eyes, and I realized that the little red plane was a toy. Sloan's toy.

"Don't tell me you have a secret fear of flying."

"Of course not." But I preferred my planes to be jumbo jets. Or at least jumbo period.

He opened the door, and I climbed over the pilot's seat and into the passenger's. "You're the one who insisted that we take the tour."

He had me there. I'd convinced him that if we didn't, someone might suspect something. And James wouldn't be pleased if Sloan didn't show me the ranch. There were bound to be questions, and since I'd already blown my cover with Sloan, I wanted to make sure that I didn't do the same with anyone else.

I buckled myself in, then gripped the edge of my seat hard.

"You are afraid of flying," Sloan said, and this time I heard the concern in his voice.

"No. Really. I have a slight aversion to heights, but it's never affected me in a plane. And I do want to see the ranch."

He sent me a smile as he turned on the engine. "I'll try not to fly too high. Just relax."

Whatever anxiety I'd been experiencing faded as the nose of the plane rose into the bright late-morning sky. The only clouds I could see were far away in the direction of the Pacific. So I wasn't prepared when a tricky patch of crosscurrents sent the little plane rocking. My heart shot to my throat and I dug my fingers into the edge of my seat.

"Easy," Sloan said. "I've got it handled."

I could see that he did, and I gradually blew out the breath I was holding.

I glanced at him. He was comfortable at the controls. It occurred to me then that he was a man who would be competent at any job he took on. I thought of the way he'd calmed Saturn on the bluff when we'd first met.

Even if he didn't come out on top in a fight or a competition, he wouldn't stay down long. Hadn't that competence and determination been a big part of what had attracted me to him from the get-go?

I forced my hands to release their grip on the seat. "I'm sorry that I'm such a coward."

The look he shot me held surprise. "You're not. Coming here to take your sister's place because you're sure that something's happened to her—that takes a kind of courage that few people would have."

His compliment warmed me and had my heart doing a little flutter. No, I thought. I was not going to go there. Heart flutters were out. It was bad enough that I had this uncontrollable chemistry with a man who belonged to my sister. I was not going to even think of letting my heart get in the mix.

Sloan leveled off the plane and banked it to the right into a circle. "If you can manage to look down, you'll treat yourself to the best view there is of the hacienda."

I made myself glance down and discovered he was right. We were directly over it, and I could see the tower reaching toward us. The sun turned the water falling from the fountain into what looked like different-colored gems. The lush green of the gardens in stark contrast to the mostly arid land surrounding the ranch gave the hacienda a fairy-tale appearance.

It was hard in the bright sunlight to believe that there were secrets here, but I knew there were. "It's a beautiful place to have such a sad history."

"How so?" Sloan asked.

"The mistresses of the Hacienda Montega don't have a very good survival rate. Beatrice took me to view the portraits in the ballroom. Only one of those women made it to her fortieth year."

"I've never given it much thought," Sloan said. "But you're right."

"I wonder if there's a curse?"

Sloan glanced at me. "Do you believe that?"

"No." But it would make a good story line. "Perhaps not a curse, but there's an interesting pattern...."

He banked the plane again and set a course for what I thought was the Pacific. As we headed over the first hills, we hit a bit of turbulence, but this time I didn't go into white-knuckle mode. It was clear that Sloan knew what he was doing. True to his word, he flew low. At times, I could even see individual cars moving along a stretch of highway. The terrain below was marked by little valleys here and there, and vast stretches of land that had been unmarred as yet by civilization.

"This property must be worth millions," I said.

"The latest offer James received for the area along the coast was a cool quarter of a billion, but they would have been willing to go higher."

I stared at him. "Why doesn't he sell?"

"Because he loves this place, and he doesn't want to see it turned into a vacation destination with malls, gas stations, golf courses and a string of high-rise hotels along the coast. I'm quoting him directly on that."

I could almost hear James saying it.

The coast came up fast, and Sloan took the plane out over the ocean before he turned and followed the coast-line. What I saw beneath me was rugged, pristine and beautiful. High cliffs bordered the Pacific, and we were flying low enough to see the power of the water as it crashed into the shore.

Out of curiosity, I asked, "What about you and Cameron? Will you respect James's wishes?"

"I would never sell." He hesitated for a moment. Then he continued. "I think I can say the same for Cameron. But she's gotten very friendly with Hal Linton, and he's connected to a group of buyers who are very interested in acquiring the property we're flying over right now."

"How long has he known her?"

"Six months or so. Since shortly after she hired Marcie." Sloan glanced at me. "Cameron isn't a fool. She wouldn't be taken in by Hal. She knew what he was about. James made sure she did."

I kept my own counsel. Of course, he might be a very good actor, but I wasn't so sure that Hal's interest in Cameron was purely monetary. But then, Marcie had almost convinced me that her interest in Austin was sincere. I couldn't discount the possibility that the brother and sister were very accomplished actors. "If James knows that Hal Linton represents a buyer, why does he allow him to be a guest at the hacienda?"

Sloan smiled then. "He likes to keep his enemies in his sights."

It was my turn to laugh then, and to my surprise, Sloan reached out and took my hand. "You have a nice laugh. I'd like to hear it more often."

My heart did that little flutter thing again. I was barely able to register it before the plane took a sudden and violent bump that had me grabbing for a handhold.

"What was that?"

Sloan didn't answer. But I got a clue when the glass

in the door to my right shattered. Someone was shooting at us.

"Get down!" Sloan shouted, unnecessarily. I'd already ducked my head as close to my knees as I could.

The plane was dropping like a rock toward the ocean and so was my stomach. Sloan swore under his breath as he struggled to get the nose back up. The swearing part wasn't good. But he was, I tried to tell myself.

"Look toward the cliffs," Sloan said in that terse tone of command that was becoming familiar to me.

Lifting my head, I did what he asked.

"Tell me what you see."

I was ready to say "the cliffs," but then I saw the dark-colored vehicle as it sped away from a spot on the cliffs behind us. "An SUV, I think. It's driving away."

What I also saw were dark plumes of smoke spiraling away behind us. When I summoned up the courage to look down, I saw that we were close, very close to the ocean. Another few yards and we were going to hit.

"Hold on," Sloan said. Sweat stood out on his forehead as he struggled with the stick in front of him, pulling it hard. The strong winds blowing in from the sea at this level had the plane pitching first one way and then the next. At one point, I was sure that I saw the spray from a wave hit the windshield.

Then suddenly, miraculously, the nose of the plane began to rise again, higher and higher. I held my breath, praying as Sloan fiddled with the controls and coaxed the plane up to the level of the cliffs. The engine coughed and sputtered. For a moment, I was sure we were going to take that long fall to the water below. Then land was coming up to meet us.

The wheels hit the ground with a vicious, teeth-jarring thud. The plane shook, shuddered, teetered to one side, and then skidded in the direction of the cliff. I held my breath. Sloan's hands remained steady as he fought to regain control. The engine sputtered one more time, went silent, and we rolled to a stop with only a few feet to spare.

I barely had time to let out the breath I was holding before we were engulfed in thick, black smoke. I tried not to breathe it in, but I must have failed because I heard myself coughing.

I felt Sloan's hands as he unstrapped me from the seat, but I could barely see him.

"C'mon." His voice was a terse command in my ear as he grabbed my hand and the backpack he'd stored behind the seat. We scrambled across the wing, jumped and hit the ground running. I didn't look back until Sloan finally stopped. The little red plane was totally engulfed in the smoke, but I didn't see any flames.

Gripping my shoulder, Sloan turned me to face him. "Are you all right? Did one of the bullets hit you?" He swore, pulled out a hankie and began to dab at my cheekbone. "You're bleeding."

"Glass," I said, remembering that the window had shattered. "I'm fine." Even as I said it, my knees went weak and a mix of shock and disbelief settled into a knot in my stomach. "Someone shot at us."

"Yeah." Sloan pulled me hard against his chest and just held me there. "You're sure it was an SUV you saw?"

"Yes." I thought about the one that I'd seen in the garage and the other that I'd driven up to the bluff the day before. Either could have been the one that I'd spotted.

He didn't say anything, but I knew that we were thinking the same thing. Sloan's arms tightened around me. For a few moments I let myself rest against him. Just until the fear subsided and I got my breath back. The steady beat of his heart soothed me, and the warmth of his body melted away the sudden chill that had engulfed me.

There was none of the heat that I'd experienced before in his arms, nothing of that all-consuming passion. Instead, I just felt as if I'd come home. Not good. Because Sloan Campbell would never be home to me. He could never be mine.

When I drew back, he regarded me steadily for a moment, then leaned down and pressed his lips gently against the scratch on my cheek. This time my heart didn't just flutter. It turned a full somersault.

Drawing back, he said, "You're right. Someone wanted Cameron out of the way."

The knots in my stomach tightened. This was one argument I would have preferred to lose.

"They want you out of the way, too." Sloan's tone was grim.

"Who?" Now that I'd finally convinced him that Cameron hadn't just taken off in a snit, I wanted his opinion. He knew these people far better than I did.

"Anyone who was at that dinner party last night and who heard James announce that I would give you a tour."

"But they wouldn't have necessarily known that you would take the plane, would they?"

"They wouldn't have to know how I'd bring you here. All they had to know was that we'd come to this spot, and it wouldn't take a rocket scientist to figure that out. Anyone who knows Cameron knows that this is her favorite place on the whole ranch. Ever since she was a little girl, she's come here. She calls it her 'gathering place.' If any place would jar her memory, this one would."

Curious, I turned to study the area, careful to keep my eyes off of the still-burning plane. We were standing near the edge of a forest that covered this portion of the ranch. The view was spectacular—lush green trees, sheer cliffs and the power of the Pacific in front of me stretching all the way to the horizon. I could see why Cameron would fall in love with this place. I could also see that it would make the perfect spot for an ambush.

"Did you come here with her?" I asked.

Sloan glanced at me. "No. She never wanted anyone with her when she came here. But I flew James out here the day after she disappeared. He was sure that she came here the morning after I argued with her."

He lifted a hand and pointed to a gap in the trees. "There's an old logging road that leads up here. It's rutted, but Cameron drove her car up here frequently."

"So someone hid in the trees and just waited for us. Someone driving an SUV."

"That doesn't narrow it down much. The ranch owns two. Austin has his own, and Doc Carter drives one, too."

Much as I tried to block it, another thought slipped into my mind. If Cameron had indeed come up here on the day she disappeared, someone could have been waiting for her, too. I knew that Sloan was thinking the same thing when his arm tightened around me.

"I'm calling the police," he said. "The car you saw may have left tracks, and they may be able to find a bullet."

16

THE EDGE OF THE CLIFF was long and rocky. Since we had half an hour to kill until the police would arrive, Sloan had suggested we walk along it to get away from the still-smoking plane. He'd also called Gus at the stables and asked him to come out and pick us up. At my curious glance, he'd explained that though James had given him a place to live after his father had left, it was Gus and Elena who'd raised him. And right now, Gus was the only person he trusted.

The breeze coming in off the water carried a fresh, salty scent, and below us I could see water hurl itself against the rocks and rise in a misty spray that now and then would split into the colors of a rainbow. My nerves were gradually settling and my mind was clearing. No wonder my sister loved this place. I would be hard-pressed to find such a solitary and peaceful spot in the madness that was L.A.

I might have been able to appreciate the spot and the view even more if most of my mind hadn't been preoccupied with trying to figure out who had shot at us. I agreed with Sloan that anyone at the ranch who knew Cameron would have known Sloan would bring me here today. Somehow, we had to find a way to narrow the list of suspects—fast.

Ahead I saw a large flat rock. When we reached it, Sloan urged me to sit down and then sat next to me. "Cameron always said that she was going to build a house right here on this spot one day. The slope of the cliff isn't as steep here, and she had plans for building stairs down to the ocean."

My throat tightened at his use of the past tense. Somehow, now that I'd convinced him that something might have happened to Cameron, the possibility was becoming more real to me. I reached for his hand. Swallowing hard, I said, "I don't want her to be…I don't want something to have happened to her. We don't know that something has."

He gave my hand a squeeze. "You're right." Then in what I was sure was an effort to change the subject, he pulled the bottle of Chardonnay, cheese and grapes out of the backpack. As he quickly and efficiently removed the cork, he suggested, "Why don't we eat while we discuss what we're going to do when we get back to the ranch."

In a matter of moments, I had a plastic glass in my hand, and a small picnic was spread out on the rock. I took a quick sip of the wine to brace myself for the upcoming battle. I was betting that Sloan would want me to stop pretending that I was Cameron, and I didn't want to. Not yet. Drawing in a deep breath, I said, "You're going to want to tell James who I really am, and I want to wait."

"I think we should wait, too."

As I stared at him in surprise, he continued, "Anything we tell him right now will only upset him. And as you just pointed out, we don't really know anything definite about what might have happened to Cameron yet."

It was one of the arguments I'd intended to use on

him, and I found it both odd and comforting that our minds would be so in tune. "The first thing we should do is to narrow the list of suspects. Whoever took that shot at us had access to an SUV and would have been absent from the house for at least an hour."

"Gus might be able to help with that. He keeps a pretty good eye on the comings and goings of the McKenzies and their houseguests."

I took a bite of cheese and glanced around the area again.

"Whoever shot at us would have to be very good with a gun. Does that eliminate anyone?"

Sloan thought for a minute. "I'm not sure about the Lintons, but hunting has traditionally been a favorite McKenzie sport. James used to take Cameron, Austin and me with him when we were younger. Doc Carter hunts, too, and I'm pretty sure that Beatrice can handle a gun."

"I'll ask my friend Pepper to check out the Lintons and see if they have any expertise with guns. They do seem to have a motive for wanting Cameron out of the way. Austin might inherit and be more amenable to selling the land."

"They'd still have to convince whomever James appointed to his board."

"But they might have a better chance of doing that with Austin. He'd probably be on their side. At least that's the way I'd see it if I were writing it."

"If you were writing it?"

"That's what I do for a living. I live in L.A. and I write plots for a soap opera, *Secrets*."

"No kidding." He poured more wine into my glass. "Tell me more about Brooke Ashby."

For another quarter of an hour, I did just that. Soon Sloan knew as much about me as anyone did—except for perhaps Pepper and my parents. The man was so easy to talk to, he'd have made a great cop or P.I. Suspects would probably line up to spill their guts to him.

The man had gotten to me. Not good, I told myself. He wasn't mine. He couldn't be mine.

But when I finished my life story, he said, "You're full of surprises, Brooke Ashby." Then he leaned over and took my mouth with his.

He might not be mine, but I definitely wanted to be his. Not good at all.

The kiss might have turned into something else, if we hadn't been interrupted by the sound of a truck rattling up the road. A second later, it broke through the woods and rolled toward us.

"Our ride." Sloan rose from the rock and walked toward it while I started packing up the picnic. By the time I finished, Gus had climbed out of the truck and was deep in conversation with Sloan. They started walking along the cliff to take a closer look at the plane. A few moments later, a state trooper's car appeared, and two officers joined Gus and Sloan at the plane.

I took a moment to move closer to the edge of the cliff. The breeze was steady and sweet. I'd always loved to be near the water. Going to the beach—even when it was one of the crowded ones on Lake Michigan or near L.A.—had always had a calming effect on me. I could see why my sister loved this place and why she'd planned to build a house here one day.

And this side of her, the part that would want to use this place as a retreat, seemed to contradict the spoiled and headstrong socialite that others had described to me. Oddly enough, I could relate to both sides of her. I might not be a socialite, but I'd left the Midwest and taken a job in Tinseltown. And we shared the need to get away from it all. When I was younger, it was riding that had helped me do that. Now I tried to hike on the weekends.

I felt as though I was gradually coming to know Cameron, and I was even starting to miss her. I wanted her to be alive. A little band tightened around my heart. Then I moved to the edge of the cliff, and my mind began to weave a story. If she'd come here on the day she disappeared, she might have been standing right where I was standing now. Sloan had said that she'd threatened to call the wedding off—a threat he hadn't taken too seriously. But I couldn't help wondering if Cameron had indeed had second thoughts about settling for a marriage that was primarily a business arrangement.

I could see why she might be torn. Her father had had a heart attack, and he was refusing to leave her everything outright. Looking around, I wondered what I might be willing to sacrifice to keep the land and to ensure that a place like this would remain as pristine as it was today.

I could picture the scene in my mind as if it were one I had written for *Secrets*. Cameron had come here alone to think it through. The sound of the surf was louder here, the wind stronger. If someone had come up behind her, would she have heard them?

Another thought occurred to me. If someone from the ranch had followed her, they wouldn't have had to sneak up, would they? If she hadn't been expecting it, it wouldn't have taken much in the way of force to make her lose her balance....

I couldn't help myself. I risked a quick look down. Just before my head began to spin and I had to raise my eyes, I thought I saw the glint of something. Directly in front of me, a seagull circled lazily on a current of air.

"Show-off," I muttered. Closing my eyes, I drew in a deep breath. Then I dropped to my knees, took a firm grip on the rocks that formed the cliff's edge and looked down again. There was definitely something on a ledge about twenty feet down, something that was reflecting sunlight.

I glanced back over my shoulder and I saw that Sloan and Gus were still in conference with the police at the plane. I dropped my gaze to the ledge, willing my eyes not to stray to the ocean below. There were all sorts of rocks and crevices to provide a handhold or foothold. And there was more of a slope to the cliff face than what I'd seen when Sloan had been flying alongside it. A talented engineer could probably find a way of attaching a set of stairs that would allow access to the beach below.

Once again, I measured the distance to the ledge and gauged the risk. I'd had to climb some pretty steep hills when I was hiking in the Hollywood Hills. This wouldn't be too much different.

Yeah, right, said a little voice in my head. I frowned, finding it interesting that my saner voice was piping up again now that Sloan Campbell wasn't around. But my inner Alice hadn't deserted me. I could make it down there, she was assuring me. I just shouldn't look down.

Without another thought, I turned, swung my legs over the edge of the cliff and felt for the first crevice with my foot. It wasn't as bad as I thought it would be. I just kept my eyes straight ahead, reminded myself that I was doing this for my long-lost twin, and climbed slowly down. Once I was on the ledge, it was a bit trickier. To minimize the problem if I had a dizzy spell, I dropped to my hands and knees.

It was then that I saw a larger crevice formed where the ledge met the cliff wall. It was large enough that I could have fit right into it. Instead, I crawled to the far end of the ledge where I'd seen the shiny object. It was a gold locket, and I thought I recognized it. I'd seen Elizabeth McKenzie wearing it in her portrait—and in the photo that Pepper had given me of Cameron.

Fear crept into me and settled in a cold, hard ball in my stomach as two scenarios played themselves out in my mind like little film clips. In one, the locket was ripped off as Cameron struggled with her attacker. In the next, she was standing at the edge of the cliff, fingering the locket as she tried to figure out what to do, and she'd torn the locket away herself when she'd been pushed. In both images, I could picture Cameron falling and striking the rocks below.

A wave of dizziness struck me with such force that my stomach pitched, and I nearly lost the little picnic lunch that I'd just enjoyed. I flattened myself on the ledge and ordered myself to breathe. I gripped the locket tightly in my hand as if by doing so I could hold on to my sister, and gradually the images faded.

The instant the dizziness eased, I knew that I had to get off the ledge. And I couldn't afford to think about it. After tucking the locket into my pocket, I inched my way back to where I'd landed. Then I drew in a deep breath and, using the crevices in the cliff wall for support, I rose to my feet and began the climb upward.

It wasn't as easy as the trip down. The wind seemed

to have picked up a bit. I thought that I could hear someone calling my name. One handhold, one foothold at a time, I told myself. It was one thing not to look down, but it was another much harder thing not to picture the distance to the rock ledge in my mind. My heart was beating fast when my hand finally clamped down on the rocks that bordered the cliff.

I felt one swift wave of relief followed by a spurt of pure panic when the rock beneath my left foot crumbled. As I dug the fingers of both hands into the cliff, I pictured rocks plummeting through the air and smacking into the foamy sea below. All the weight of my body was on my weak ankle. A wave of dizziness hit me, and for a moment I felt myself teeter. I was going to fall.

A hand grabbed my wrist. A second later another hand joined the first and I felt myself being hauled upward. The moment that my feet were on solid ground, Sloan's hands gripped my shoulders and he gave me a hard shake.

I opened my eyes to see fear in his.

"Are you all right? What happened? Did you fall?"

"No. I climbed down because I saw something."

He gave me another shake and fury joined the fear in his eyes.

"I found something." Reaching into my pocket, I pulled out the locket. "It was on the ledge. It's hers, isn't it?"

Sloan took the locket. "Yes. She wore this every day."

"Someone pushed her. It must have torn off in the struggle. I—"

I couldn't go on. There was something in my throat that stopped me. A sob. I didn't realize it, but I must have been crying because Sloan pulled me abruptly against his chest and just held me close. I might have been able to pull myself together if he hadn't done that. I'd been so certain that Cameron was alive—I still wanted to believe that she was. I wanted to be able to get to know her, to love her. And then I thought of Sloan and I held on to him even tighter and wept for both our loss.

IT WAS MORE THAN AN HOUR later before we got back to the ranch. The troopers had found some tire tracks and they'd remained at the scene to make plaster casts.

Sloan was angry with me. On the ride back to the hacienda, he barely said a word to me. At least Gus hadn't overheard my outburst about Cameron. He'd still been inspecting the damage to the plane when Sloan had realized I was missing and the older man had stayed with the troopers.

Once I'd recovered from my weep-a-thon, I'd tried to convince myself that the two scenes I'd pictured so vividly in my mind could be worst-case scenarios. Finding the locket on the cliff didn't necessarily mean that Cameron had fallen over. There could be other explanations.

Along with my inner Alice, I also had an inner Little Mary Sunshine. I didn't want to give up on Cameron yet.

But it wasn't looking good.

Now that I'd gotten a bit of a grip on myself, I was willing to concede that Sloan might have a reason to be upset with me. I'd taken a risk climbing down to the ledge. But I'd found Cameron's locket. That had to count for something. We now had proof that Cameron had been to the cliff, and that something had happened to make her drop it.

When Gus finally pulled his truck to a stop at the stables, Sloan told me to go up to the main house. He'd be up as soon as he and Gus made arrangements for the plane. Then they disappeared into Sloan's office. I didn't much like being dismissed as if I were a disobedient child. Still, I started to do just what he'd said—partly because I'd been raised to be a "good girl." One of the reasons I was growing to like Cameron was because I sensed that she had a little more of the "bad girl" in her than I did.

Then there was the fact that the day had been an eventful one. I'd had mind-blowing sex, nearly lost my life in a plane crash, faced my biggest fear by climbing down to that ledge, and then indulged in a crying jag.

Okay, so it was only twenty feet to the cliff. I'd still done it. And I'd found Cameron's locket. Going up to the hacienda would give me some time to figure out what it meant.

Or I could battle Hannibal over who the bed really belonged to and take a nap.

Both of those options disappeared the instant I saw Marcie, Austin and Hal coming out of one of the stable doors.

"There you are," Marcie called. "I told Austin you hadn't forgotten we were going riding."

Truth be told, I had. Completely. I tried to glance at my watch unobtrusively, and found that it was a little after three. Time flies when you're being shot down out of the sky.

"We had your horse saddled for you," Marcie added.

I thought of the promise I'd made to Sloan that I wouldn't go off with any one of them alone. But this was a group. Surely, there was safety in numbers. Besides, time was of the essence, and if I went with them, I might be able to find out more about Cameron's disappearance.

Hal and Austin each led a saddled horse, and Marcie was leading two. Doc Carter and Beatrice brought up the rear of the little parade, sans horses.

"You haven't changed your mind, have you?" Marcie asked.

I hesitated for one more instant. But when the horse neighed softly and pushed her nose into my shoulder, I was immediately won over. Hadn't I been longing for a ride ever since I'd first stood on that bluff and seen the horses?

"Of course, I haven't changed my mind." I smiled at Marcie and took the reins she held out to me. Then I turned to Beatrice and Doc Carter. "Will you be joining us?"

Doc Carter chuckled. "Not today. Austin and Marcie wanted us to see the horses that the Radcliffs are turning over to us. You young ones go off and enjoy yourselves." He took my hand and patted it. "Perhaps we can get together when you get back."

"Sure."

"See you then."

Hal and Austin were already seated by the time I put my foot in the stirrup and mounted my horse. She was a beauty and as I leaned over to pat her neck, I asked Marcie, "What's her name?"

"Oh, sorry. I keep forgetting about the amnesia. Her name is Lace Ribbons. You call her Lacey."

I patted her neck. "You're a beauty, Lacey." And she was. She was black as pitch with not a brown hair on her. And she had a dainty air about her. I thought of Saturn and felt that they might make a perfect match.

"You've had her since she was a two-year-old. You never ride any other mount," Marcie said.

Austin and Hal were leading the way out of the stable yard, and we fell in behind them.

"Why don't I ride any other horse?" I asked.

Marcie glanced at me. "I never thought much about it. But you confessed to me once that you'd been thrown off a horse as a child, and you'd been careful about your mounts ever since. Lace Ribbons has perfect manners."

I didn't doubt that she did. But I was thinking of Saturn.

I saw that Austin and Hal were leading us toward the area of the ranch behind the hacienda and its gardens. I searched the map I'd made in my mind on the bluff the day before and recalled that a stream, bordered by woods, wound its way through this part of the property.

Sure enough, Austin urged his horse into a trot and started toward the stream. It had been so long since I'd ridden that I was yearning for a fast run. I was about to say so to Marcie when she moved her horse forward and Austin fell back.

I bit back a sigh and managed a smile for my "cousin." I had a hunch that the Lintons and Austin had an agenda that didn't include the gallop I was longing for.

"I want to apologize for my behavior last night," he said as soon as he drew alongside me.

To my surprise, I heard a note of sincerity in his tone and read it in his expression. "No apology needed. I'm sure that my sudden return must have been a…" I paused to search for the right word. "…a bit of a shock to you."

Austin met my eyes steadily. "I'm happy to know that you're all right. It's just…"

"That you've been doing very well in the business and you think now that I'm back, that will change."

"I know it will." There was anger in his tone. His jaw tensed, and his knuckles whitened on the hand holding the reins. "Everything will go back to the way it was."

Austin's horse, sensing the anger, moved restlessly beneath him, and I became aware suddenly of the fact that my cousin and I were virtually alone. We'd ridden more deeply into the woods and we were going even more slowly now, following the winding path of the stream. Marcie and Hal had moved ahead and trees blocked them from my sight.

"Why don't you tell me why you think everything will change now," I said.

"Because Uncle James doesn't trust me. Now that you're back and you're marrying Sloan, I'll go back to babysitting a desk. He's never given me the kind of chance I deserve."

He sounded a bit like a whining child. "Why not?"

"Because my father had a gambling problem and embezzled hundreds of thousands of dollars while he was running the ranch. No one suspected anything until he died of a heart attack on one of those riverboat gambling cruises."

I made a mental note to tell Pepper that the mystery of Beatrice's disappearing husband had been solved. "That doesn't have anything to do with you."

"It shouldn't. But Uncle James is big on bloodlines. You're his blood. And he figures I've inherited my father's bad genes. Add that to the fact that I've never been able to compete with you and Sloan. I have as much McKenzie blood in me as you do, but I'm not good enough to be trusted with any responsibility."

I studied him for a moment, putting what he'd just told me together with what Marcie had said and with what Pepper had written in her report. "I've been told that you like gambling better than you like to work."

Color flushed Austin's face. Once again, I saw his knuckles whiten. Clearly, my cousin had anger management issues. "I've made mistakes. I know that. While I was in college, I figured if everyone thought I was like my father, I might as well live up to the name. But things have changed since I met Marcie. I've changed, and I've made a fresh start. I know I didn't make a good impression last night, but that was...not me."

"Marcie says that you haven't had that much to drink in a long time."

He met my eyes. "My reformation began when you hired her six months ago. She's made me see things differently because she sees me differently. No one has ever believed in me the way Marcie does. She's helped me to change."

He was in love with her. I could see it in his eyes, hear it in his voice. Did he have any idea that Marcie's interest in reforming him might be motivated by the possibility of his coming into a great deal of money and land? And if Marcie was so intent on helping Austin change his ways, why had she been with him in Vegas on the very day that Cameron had disappeared?

"Look. I've done a good job in the last month. You can even ask Uncle James about that. All I want is the chance to continue."

In spite of the questions and suspicions spinning

around in my head, I really wanted to believe Austin. There was the possibility that he'd been taken in by the Lintons and that he was just a pawn in a bigger game the sister and brother were playing. But there was also the possibility that Austin was his father's son and was trying to con me. In my mind, I could picture the story line going either way. And if Austin *was* trying to con me, my best bet was to let him think he'd been successful.

"I don't see that as a problem," I said.

A mixture of relief and hope washed over his face. "You'll give me a chance then?"

I reached out and covered his hand with mine. "Of course, I will."

"Thanks, Cam." He looked so pleased as he leaned over to brush a kiss on my cheek that I felt a twinge of guilt. "I won't disappoint you."

What was he going to think when he found out who I really was and that my assurances meant squat?

As Austin urged his horse forward to join Marcie again, my cell phone rang. I dug it out of my pocket and checked the caller ID. Pepper. I reined in Lace Ribbons. "What have you got?"

"Hello to you, too," Pepper said with a laugh.

"I'm out riding the range," I explained. Well, not really, I thought as I glanced around. As we'd followed the stream, it had widened and the forest had dropped back a bit from the bank. There was still plenty of room for the horses, but trees effectively hemmed us in from the open country.

"You have company I take it, so I'll be brief. Cole checked in Las Vegas, and Austin and Marcie were both seen in a restaurant and at the gaming tables. One of the croupiers remembers that Austin lost about ten thousand dollars. However, no one was able to verify that Hal was with them."

"Interesting," I said. It meant that Austin hadn't been quite truthful about his reformation. He'd been gambling on the day that Cameron had disappeared. It also meant that Hal didn't have an alibi for that day. Ahead of me Austin and Marcie urged their horses into a trot and disappeared around a bend. Hal turned his horse around and headed toward me.

"Beatrice was indeed at the flower show in San Diego," Pepper said. "Several people saw her there. She gave a speech at the luncheon."

So that leaves Sloan, James, Doc Carter and Hal Linton without alibis. "Any chance you could find out if either of the Lintons have any expertise with guns?" I asked in a low voice as Hal slowly but surely closed the distance between us. Through the trees to my right, I saw that Marcie and Austin had veered off from the path we'd been following and were probably headed out of the woods.

"Sure, but I don't like the sound of that."

What I didn't like was the fact that I'd once more been outmaneuvered by the Lintons. Unless I wanted to turn tail and run back the way we'd come, I was now alone in an isolated area with a man who had no alibi for the day my sister had disappeared. A man who might have a very good reason for wanting her to disappear.

17

"I'M SORRY FOR LAST NIGHT," Hal said as he reined to a stop directly in front of me.

No, I decided. I was not going to turn around and run. Mallory Carstairs certainly wouldn't and I didn't think Cameron would, either. Besides, this was my chance to learn more about the man my sister had kissed in the garden the night before she'd gone missing. "This seems to be my day for getting apologies."

He had the grace to wince a bit. "Austin and I both behaved poorly last night."

I couldn't help but wonder if behaving badly was an aberration for Hal Linton, too. I thought it might be. The man had all the marks of one smooth operator. He reminded me a bit of a character on *Secrets* who managed to always come out on top.

Studying Hal, I tried to see him as Cameron might have seen him. With that dark hair, tanned skin and good bones, he was handsome in a pretty way that Sloan wasn't. Hal's features were smooth while Sloan's were rugged. Hal was sleekly groomed, his hair neatly trimmed. Sloan looked as if he was long overdue to see his barber. I remembered how it had felt to run my hands through that hair and of how messed up it had looked when we'd just finished making love. Heat crept into my cheeks.

Hal dismounted and held up his hand. "Why don't we rest the horses and walk for a bit?"

I hesitated, looking to my right, but Marcie and Austin had completely disappeared.

"Please," he said. "This is a place that we came to more than once. Doc Carter thought it might help you remember."

Curious now, I held out my hand and dismounted. Hal's palm was soft and smooth with none of the calluses that were on Sloan's. He was a more sophisticated dresser, too. Last night, he'd worn Armani, and I knew that the golf shirt and riding breeches he wore today had designer labels. There was a sheen of money and sophistication here. This was a man who'd court a woman carefully with flowers, champagne, elegant restaurants. As a lover, he'd be both smooth and skilled.

If Sloan wanted a woman, I didn't think he'd bother with all that. In fact, he hadn't. In my mind, I pictured him standing in the archway to his kitchen and the way he'd looked at me when he'd closed the distance between us. He'd had me right then. But later, he'd provided the romance. I thought of our picnic on that flat rock in Cameron's favorite place.

"Cameron?"

"What?" Dragging my thoughts back, I turned to see Hal looking at me in an odd sort of way.

"Are you all right? Are you remembering something? Do you want me to take you back to the ranch?"

"I'm fine," I said. At least I would be if I could stop thinking about Sloan Campbell. I'd been away from him for—what?—twenty minutes, but I couldn't get him out of my mind. Ridiculous. I should be thinking of finding out what this man might know about my sister's disappearance. "What did you just say?"

"Does this bring back any memories?" He gestured to the space around us, and for the first time I took it in. We'd walked into a little clearing. The stream widened a bit here, and wildflowers grew along its border. Their scent filled the air, and there was a place just ahead of us where a cluster of trees offered complete privacy. "It's lovely."

"But you don't remember anything?"

I met his eyes and saw that he was studying me very intently. "I don't remember ever being here before."

There was a tightening in his jaw that I didn't like. So there was temper beneath that smooth-as-silk facade. While I found it interesting, I didn't much like the fact that I'd let myself be manipulated into being alone with him. He was even carrying my horse's reins.

Drawing in a deep breath, he said, "I don't want to pressure you. Doc Carter said that's the worst thing I could do."

"What exactly do you want, Hal?"

"I want you to remember what we meant to each other, what we were before you went away."

To my surprise, it wasn't just temper I saw, but pain and perhaps regret. Had Hal Linton actually been in love with Cameron? Had she been in love with him? Was that what she had gone to the cliffs to think about? I wanted to know.

"What exactly were we to each other?" I asked.

Hal looked at me for a moment. "Do you know how

hard it is for me to see you standing there, to hear you say that you can't remember me? We were…friends. I wanted more. You didn't. But that was going to change."

"Why?"

"Because you were having second thoughts about marrying Sloan."

"I told you that?"

"Yes. Several times. You told me that the night before you disappeared, the night that your fiancé eavesdropped on us and caught us kissing in the garden."

Something knotted in my stomach.

He gripped my shoulders. His hands might have been smooth, but they were strong. I felt a skip of panic.

"You're in danger. I sensed it that night. I should have done something. If I had…" He broke off, releasing me as if he'd just realized he'd grabbed hold of me. He ran a hand through his hair. "Sorry. I promised myself that I wouldn't touch you."

He turned and paced a few steps away, as if he had to keep his distance if he was going to keep his promise. "I'm going to tell you something that I didn't tell you before you left. When I ran into you at the Derby, it wasn't by accident. I was hired by the group of investors who have approached your father with an offer to buy this place. My job was to make contact with you, to get close to you. Hell, I was supposed to use any means I could—including seduction—to convince you to persuade your father to sell the place."

"The surprise announcement of my engagement to Sloan must have thrown a spanner into the works."

Through the tan I could see a flush stain his cheeks.

"I'm not proud now of what I had planned to do. At

the time, when my associates proposed the job, it seemed easy enough. It paid well, and I found you attractive. That was the kind of man I was before I met you. Everything changed then. The last six months we've had fun together. You're different than other women for me. We'd become friends. You confided in me. And I fell in love with you."

I didn't say anything. I couldn't speak for Cameron. And I wasn't quite sure that he was telling the truth. He looked sincere enough, but the man had to be an accomplished liar to have gotten where he was in life.

"I won't tell you that you felt the same way," Hal said.

I raised my brows. "Isn't that exactly what you tried to do last night?"

His face reddened even more. "I was worried about you. You have amnesia, for God's sake. I wanted to give you some reason for not being swept up in James's plans again. Believe the worst about me. But I want you to know that you were having second thoughts about your upcoming marriage on the night before you disappeared."

He took a step toward me, but kept his hands at his sides. "Don't marry him, Cameron. For your own sake, wait at least until you get your memory back and can remember why it was that you felt you had to run away from here."

Once again, I couldn't think of anything to say. Everything he said made sense, and his account of what had happened in the garden matched Sloan's. Was he confessing all this because he was concerned about my safety? Or was he doing it on purpose to confuse me?

Marcie, Austin and Hal all seemed perfectly fooled by my impersonation. They believed that I was

Cameron McKenzie suffering from amnesia. The person who'd been suspicious of me from the get-go was Sloan. Was that because he knew what had really happened to Cameron?

No. I didn't believe that. He'd been in that plane with me. Both of us could have been killed. My head began to spin, and I pressed a hand to my temple. Not because I was suspicious of Sloan, I wasn't. It had just been an eventful day. I'd been shot down in a plane, nearly toppled off a cliff.

"Something is wrong." Hal took my arm. "I'll take you back to Doc Carter."

"No. I'm fine. I—" I broke off when I heard hoof-beats approaching, and I knew before I turned that it would be Sloan and Saturn. I could feel the anger radiating off him in waves as he reined in Saturn and dismounted. But his voice was controlled and it was Hal he addressed when he reached us.

"Your sister and Austin are waiting for you. James sent me to bring Cameron back. He needs to see her."

Sloan's tone was even, pleasant almost, but it was clear that Hal was being dismissed.

Hal turned to me, a worried expression on his face. "I'll stay if you like."

"No." I didn't glance at Sloan. I knew he'd have that mocking look in his eyes. "I have something that I want to talk to Sloan about before we go back."

Hal's expression changed, lightened. "Good. That's good." He gave Sloan a nod before he mounted his horse. "See you in a bit then."

Sloan waited until Hal was out of sight and earshot before he turned to me and even then he kept his voice low. "You promised that you wouldn't go off alone with any of them."

"I didn't go off alone. There were four of us." Okay, technically, I knew I was on shaky ground.

"I only counted two when I got here." His voice might have been under control, but there was anger in his eyes and in the way he grabbed my arm to lead me toward the horses. "C'mon."

"Wait just a minute." I dug in my heels. Maybe it was the culmination of the dramatic events of the day, or maybe it was because I felt I was being lectured like a child, but my own temper rose to meet his. "I came here to try to find out what happened to my sister. I can't do that if I'm confined to the house. Austin, Marcie and Hal all have reasons to want Cameron to disappear."

"Which is exactly why it was reckless and stupid of you to go off riding with them."

"Stupid?" I used my free hand to poke him in the chest.

"Yes, stupid."

I poked him again. "Stupid was sitting around for five weeks without even wondering if something had happened to Cameron."

I saw in his eyes that my comment had struck home.

"Okay—you've got a point. But you've convinced me that Cameron is at the very least in trouble. And so are you. The plane nearly crashed. You nearly fell off that cliff. I came close to losing you twice, and then I learn you've gone off riding with three of the people who might have been responsible for Cameron's disappearance!" Sloan grabbed my shoulders and gave me a shake. "Which is why you're going to go back to the house and stay put until we figure out who's behind all this."

He'd raised his voice, so I did, too. "Until we figure this out, *we* includes me. I'm not going to cower in my room. I came here to find my sister, and you're not going to stop me!"

His eyes were bright angry slits. "You're just like her—stubborn, unreasonable—"

"I'm not Cameron."

He gave me another shake. "No, you're not. She could never push me this far. No one could. No one but you."

His mouth crushed down on mine, and in one fluid move I was beneath him on the ground. Passion erupted with such force, such speed. Was this what had been simmering inside of him since he'd pulled me to safety off that ledge? Was this what had been simmering inside of me?

Those hands could be so gentle. This time they weren't. This time he was relentless. Those hard, calloused fingers ran over my skin in that meticulous way he had, scraping, setting new fires and fueling the ones that were already burning.

This is what I'd been craving—the fury, the fire, the freedom. I yanked at his shirt, pulling it free of his jeans and ran my hands up his back, exploring the steely strength of those muscles.

Roughly, he bit my bottom lip and more flames shot to life inside of me. I could feel everything—the hard ground beneath my back, the sharp press of pebbles through the thin silk of my blouse. With each breath, I drew in the scent of wildflowers, horses and Sloan. I saw the play of light and shadow over my closed eyelids.

And his taste—I couldn't seem to get enough of the endless flavors that I found each time he kissed me. There was always something new, some elusive nuance that I hadn't sampled before. This time I tasted anger, but there was also desire—hot, dark, restless. And addicting.

My whole world narrowed to this moment, to him, to us and what we could bring each other.

He rolled over suddenly so that I was straddling him and he began work on my clothes, pulling the buttons loose. I heard the erotic sound of silk tearing as I struggled with his belt. Once I yanked his shirt up, he rose to help me pull it off. We discarded clothes, hands grasping, groping, fumbling, growing more and more desperate.

Free at last, he rolled me beneath him again and took his hands on another lethal journey. I thought he'd shown me everything before, but he unveiled more secrets as he began to use his mouth on me.

Each one of my muscles melted, my bones liquefied, and one shudder after another racked my body as Sloan took his lips and teeth on a journey down my torso, my stomach and inner thigh and finally up again. He was taking things from me, things I'd never get back, and I only wanted to give him more.

My fingers were digging into his shoulders, my voice crying out his name when he finally put his mouth to my center. The climax slammed into me, a hard, bare-fisted punch that sent me flying higher and higher into a spiral that it seemed I might never come out of. I was still shuddering when he rose over me to sheathe himself in the condom.

I should have been sated, but I wanted more.

He positioned himself between my legs, then framed my face with his hands. "I want you."

"Take me," I said.

He thrust into me, quick and hard, and then we began

to move piston quick. With each second, with each thrust, there was more and more pleasure, seemingly endless until we shot headlong over that final airless peak—and shattered.

AFTERWARD, WE LAY TOGETHER on the ground. Somehow, I'd ended up sprawled across his chest with no clear memory of how I'd gotten there. My head rested on his shoulder, my hand on his chest. I could feel his heart beat fast and steady beneath my hand, hear the sound of his breathing in my ear. Above that came the sound of the stream, the rustle of leaves. Inexplicably, I felt at home.

And I shouldn't. I couldn't. Still, I let myself drift, savoring the feeling. When I finally stirred, I felt his arms tighten around me for a second before he let me raise my head and meet his eyes.

"Who won?" I asked.

Sloan's lips curved in one of those rare smiles as he pulled some twigs out of my hair. "The fight? I did."

My eyes narrowed. "In your dreams. Want to go another round?"

He laughed and I felt my heart do that little flutter thing again. It was happening more frequently, and I was going to have to think about it. Just not now.

"I'm not sure I'm up to it," he said as he sat up and settled me more comfortably on his lap. Then his expression sobered and something like regret slid into his eyes. Lifting a hand, he tucked my hair behind my ears. "What am I going to do with you, Brooke Ashby?"

He was talking about more than settling our argument, but I pretended that was what he'd meant.

"How about a compromise? You want me to stay in my room, and I need to keep investigating what happened to Cameron. I've already made people uncomfortable."

The sound he made was close to a snort. "You've done more than that. Someone shot our plane down. And the minute I turn my back, the Lintons and Austin have spirited you away. I want to call off your whole masquerade."

I drew in a deep breath and summoned up all of my debate skills. "Just give me until tomorrow night. As long as everyone thinks I'm Cameron, we have a better chance of learning something."

"And you have a better chance of getting hurt."

I turned and met his eyes steadily. "If it turns out that I'm James's biological daughter, I might be in just as much danger as Cameron was."

For a moment, Sloan's arms tightened around me. Then they relaxed. "I wish to hell that I didn't agree with you."

Pushing my advantage, I said, "How about we work together until we figure it out? I won't spend another minute out of your sight."

He considered that for a minute. "I took you up in the plane and nearly got us both killed."

"We weren't killed thanks to you."

He was on the brink of agreeing with me, so I summoned up all my debate skills. "Even if you lock me in my room, I'll find a way to get out. I'm only on the second floor. I've had experience tying bedsheets together and rappelling down walls."

He studied me. "For a woman who's afraid of heights, you've picked up some interesting skills."

I nearly had him. "You were right earlier. I am stubborn. I'm not going to give up on this, and two heads are better then one." I gave him a quick kiss. "It means that we'd spend more time together, and I'd owe you big-time."

The corners of his mouth curved. "Are we talking about sexual favors?"

I smiled at him. "I certainly hope so."

Sloan framed my face with his hands and ran his thumbs gently over my cheekbones. "Okay, but I want your word that you won't go off on your own again."

"You've got it. And I want yours that we share all information. Like what you were doing in your office with Gus while I was riding out here with the Lintons and Austin."

"I told Gus and he'll tell Elena who you really are, and I brought Gus up to speed on what we now believe about Cameron's disappearance." He pressed his fingers to my lips. "I told you before that I trust Gus, and we can trust Elena, too. They'll watch our backs."

"Okay. I guess we could use that."

"Gus is checking into who might have used that SUV this morning, and he'll keep tabs on comings and goings. Elena can be our eyes and ears in the house. What did you learn from the Lintons and Austin?"

"Not much. They're either totally innocent or they're accomplished liars."

I filled him in on the update Pepper had given me on the alibis, as well as what I'd discovered during the ride. "Austin sounds like he really wants a chance to prove that he's not his father's son. And Hal—I hate to say it—but he's got me almost believing that he really fell for Cameron."

"That might explain why she was kissing him in the

garden," he said. "But both Austin and Hal have every reason in the world to lie to you. And Hal doesn't have an alibi for the day Cameron disappeared. They could be working together."

I smiled ruefully. "There's that, of course."

"You have a soft heart, Brooke Ashby."

"Did Cameron?" I asked, suddenly hungry to know more about my twin.

Sloan thought for a moment. "She had a tougher outer shell than you. And she wasn't above running a few cons herself. She had a lot of James in her."

As we talked about Cameron in the past tense again, I felt my throat tightening. "In spite of everything we've learned today, I can't think of Cameron as being dead. I've had this feeling all along that she's in trouble, and that I had to do something about it—fast. But I never had the feeling that she was dead."

Sloan tipped my chin up so that our eyes met. "We'll find out."

The words and his simple faith in them cheered me. "And isn't it convenient that we have all the prime suspects gathered together in one house—just like in an Agatha Christie novel?" Another thought struck me. "And we owe that to James. The wily old fox."

"What do you mean?" Sloan asked.

"Scheduling the wedding for tomorrow was a perfect excuse to keep everyone here. If he hadn't done that, Marcie and Hal and Austin would have gone right back to Saratoga Springs. The races and the parties have another week to run."

"Yeah, you're right. I've been wondering just what James's role is in all of this."

"You're not thinking he was involved in Cameron's disappearance?"

"No. But it's just like him to find a way to keep everyone here and try to stir something up. You're like him in that way."

That surprised me. "I am?"

His brows shot up. "You came here masquerading as your sister with a story of memory loss. I'd call that a sure-fire recipe for stirring things up. And you've succeeded."

With that he shifted me to the ground, rose to his feet and held out a hand.

I found myself reluctant to take it. Once we were back at the hacienda, I'd have to start thinking again and planning. Who should I talk to? What kinds of questions should I ask? And I'd have to think about Sloan. What we had was temporary, I wasn't going to lie to myself about that. And I could feel the minutes I had with him ticking away.

"C'mon," Sloan said. "We can rinse off in the stream before we ride back."

The moment I was on my feet, he scooped me up in his arms, carried me into the stream, and when the water reached his waist, abruptly let me go. Then to top it off, he placed a hand on my head and shoved me under.

I was sputtering when I finally surfaced. And Sloan was laughing. It took me two tries to get my feet under me, and he rewarded me by cupping water in both hands and throwing it in my face. I choked, lost my footing and went under again. When I came up, I saw that he'd gone into fresh gales of laughter.

My heart did more than a flutter this time. It went into a full-fledged somersault. I pressed my hand against my chest. This serious, enigmatic man I'd been fascinated with from the first time I'd seen his picture had just dropped me in a stream and purposely dunked me.

It was while I was watching him, his head thrown back, the sound of his laugh filling the air around us, that I admitted to myself what I'd been trying to deny since the first time I'd looked into his eyes. I could fall in love with Sloan Campbell.

A mix of panic and joy swirled through me. Talk about complications. I had no idea how to plot my way out of this. And since I didn't want to think about it and was barely ready to accept it, I decided that I could at least get even with him. Drawing in a deep breath, I slipped under the water, then pushed off in his direction. Circling around, I came up behind him, grabbed one of his feet and yanked it hard. Looking up through the water, I saw his arms flail and then he pitched forward like a felled tree.

Of course, my revenge would have been more perfect if I could have escaped unscathed. But he twisted, grabbed my waist and pulled me close. In the wavering shafts of light piercing the gray water, he looked like some kind of sea god, and I wanted him as fiercely as I had such a short time before.

As if he'd read my mind, he kissed me. Sensations shot through me—the chill of the water, the heat of his mouth and hands. The hardness of his fingers at my waist, the soft, thorough movement of his tongue on mine.

Suddenly we were shooting upward. Sloan dragged his mouth from mine, and we both drew in huge gulps of air.

"We could have drowned."

"We might yet," he said as he lifted me and positioned my legs around him. "I want you." Suiting actions to words, he pushed into me. But it wasn't far enough. I tightened my legs around him and tried to wiggle closer.

"Hold on tight."

I thought then that he was going to move to the bank of the stream, but instead, he withdrew and pushed in again, withdrew and pushed in again, teasing me. When he withdrew the third time, he paused. "I don't have a condom."

"I'm on the pill."

His gaze narrowed. "Are you involved with someone back in L.A.?"

"No. I like to be prepared."

"Good." He thrust into me this time all the way. "That's good."

I couldn't have agreed more. Then we both began to move. The water was working against us, slowing us down, keeping the ultimate pleasure just out of reach until I thought I would simply go mad.

"Now." Sloan's voice was hoarse, his fingers digging into my hips. "Come with me, Brooke."

When he thrust into me, I did.

18

THE AFTERNOON SUN was low in the sky and the shadows long when Sloan finally gave me a leg up onto Lace Ribbons. I felt both guilt and reluctance as I settled myself in the saddle. Guilt because we'd tarried longer than we probably should have. With each moment that passed, my "wedding day" was getting closer, and my masquerade would be over. So would the best chance I had of finding out what had happened to Cameron. I glanced back at the stream. In spite of that, I was reluctant to let go of this time that I'd spent together with Sloan. How would I feel when I had to leave Sloan forever?

As if he'd read my mind—which I was beginning to think he could—he laid a hand over mine. "We have to talk about us."

Panic skittered up my spine. I thought I knew what he wanted to tell me, and I didn't want to hear it yet. "First things first. We have to find out what happened to Cameron."

His hand tightened on mine before he released me. "Then we're coming back here where we can be alone. Promise me."

"All right." I managed a smile. "Although this is

not the safest place to come. We nearly drowned twice by my count."

"Nonsense. You just need a little practice building up the time you can hold your breath. I'd be glad to help you."

"Oh, really? The way I recall it I nearly had to use CPR on you that last time we went under."

He was laughing as he untied Saturn.

I was finding this new playful side of Sloan delightful. Inspired by it, I called, "I'll beat you to the stables." Without waiting for him to mount up, I loosened my hold on the reins and used my heels on Lace Ribbons.

She responded beautifully, springing into a canter that took us quickly out of the trees. Then at my urging she accelerated into a full gallop. I leaned over her and said, "We have a head start, girl. Let's make the most of it."

If we'd started out together, Saturn and Sloan would have left us in the dust, but with the handicap I'd given us, we might have a chance. "C'mon Lacey." Air parted, then whipped past us and the ground fell away beneath us. I could hear hoofbeats now. Sloan and Saturn were gaining on us.

If I stayed on the route that Austin had chosen, there would be no contest. So instead, I bided my time and tried a surprise. When Sloan was nearly on me, I veered right and headed for a fence. He'd have to check his momentum to follow me, and that would buy me some time.

"C'mon, Lacey," I crooned to her. "Show me what you can do." I bent over her as she raced forward. The fence was only about ten yards away when I felt the saddle slip to the right. I leaned hard to my left, trying to compensate. But the horse faltered, unsettled by the shift in balance. Panicked, she reared up. Dropping the reins, I grabbed for her mane and kicked free of the stirrups. She reared up again, and when she came down this time, she bucked, lunged forward, and I hurtled over her head.

Time seemed to slow while I was airborne. My whole life didn't flash before my eyes but I did manage to conjure up an image of my first riding instructor. A tall man with the build of Ichabod Crane, his constant advice to me had been to tuck and roll. I tried, but when I rolled my head smacked hard into something. Stars exploded and the world went black.

I KEPT MY EYES CLOSED because the pounding behind them was more muted then. I could hear Sloan's voice. He was talking in that soft, authoritative tone that was becoming so familiar to me. The other voice belonged to James, and his tone was angry but hushed, so I couldn't make the words out. Or maybe I just didn't want to put in the effort.

Sloan had carried me to James's suite of rooms as soon as we'd arrived at the ranch. The trip back was pretty much a blur because I kept drifting in and out of consciousness. Now I wanted very much to sleep. To escape.

Cool fingers closed over my wrist. "Don't go to sleep, Cameron."

The knife-sharp pain in my head became more intense. As did the memory of my mad race across the field toward the fence, the slipping saddle and the breath-stealing impact of my body slamming into the ground. Pushing the images away, I tried to sit up and firm hands settled on my shoulders.

"Not yet."

I opened my eyes and found myself looking into Doc Carter's. He released my wrist and began to shine a small light into my eyes. "Her eyes look fine. Her pulse is steady."

"You don't have to talk about me as if I'm not in the room."

Doc Carter held up three fingers. "How many?"

"Three."

"Who's the current president of the United States?"

"George Bush. With a *W* in the middle."

Doc nodded at me. "Fine. And what's your name?"

I opened my mouth and caught myself just before I said Brooke. "Cameron McKenzie."

He smiled down at me. "So far so good. It's been a long time since you were unseated by a horse, young lady."

Then abruptly, it wasn't Doc Carter's face leaning over mine. It was Sloan's.

"How do you feel?" His face was drawn with worry, and his mouth was set in a grim line.

Suddenly worried myself, I wiggled toes, fingers. "Is anything broken except my head?"

"No. I checked you out pretty thoroughly before I moved you."

"I don't see any signs of a concussion," Doc Carter said. "But I could drive her into San Diego."

"No." Sloan and I spoke in unison.

I levered myself into a sitting position and managed not to wince. "I'm not going to a hospital. I had my fill of them after my mugging." And I had less than twenty-four hours left to find out what had happened to Cameron. "I just fell off a horse. I'll live." And then I remembered. "The saddle…"

"The girth was cut," Sloan said as he took one of my hands in his. "The run created too much stress and it tore the rest of the way."

I gripped Sloan's hand tighter, but I kept my gaze on Doc Carter. "Who saddled my horse?"

His eyes widened. "I don't know."

"You were there. You and Beatrice came out of the stable with Austin and the Lintons."

Now Carter was frowning. "Beatrice, Austin and the Lintons were in the stables when I arrived. A call had come in for Austin and Elena asked me to deliver the message. The horses were already saddled when I got there."

"I'll have Gus check into it," Sloan said.

"Well." Doc Carter closed his bag. "I want you to take it easy for the next day or so. Don't go to sleep for a while."

I made the mistake of nodding and pain sliced into my head again. "Aspirin?"

He took a bottle out of his case and shook two pills into my palm. I swallowed both of them dry before he handed me a glass of water.

Doc turned toward James. "Shall I tell Beatrice to hold dinner for you?"

"No," James directed. "Tell her to go ahead and serve dinner without us. Elena will bring something up when we're ready."

None of us spoke again until Doc Carter left the room. Then Sloan looked at me. "We're going to tell James everything."

I opened my mouth, but Sloan held up a hand. "First someone shoots at you, then your saddle girth is cut. I'm putting a stop to your masquerade right now."

"No need to argue about it," James said. "I already know who she is. She's Brooke Ashby, and she's here because I sent her that letter telling her that she was adopted."

MINUTES LATER, I was still trying to absorb what James had revealed. He'd forestalled questions, insisting that Sloan pour us each some of the brandy he kept in his desk.

I waited for Sloan to sit down beside me before I asked the question that was foremost in my mind. "Do you know what happened to Cameron?"

"Yes, I know." His face and his tone were grim. "But what I say stays in this room. Agreed?"

"All right." I nodded.

Sloan looked angry. "I'm not promising anything."

James studied him for a minute. "Her life and Cameron's life might depend on your silence."

"She's alive then?" I linked my fingers with Sloan's. "Where?"

James took a sip of his brandy. "She's safe in L.A. I've hired security for her."

"So she did run away," Sloan said. "And you knew all the while where she was."

"I knew where she was. But she didn't run away. The morning after you quarreled, she went to that spot she loves so much by the ocean. She told me that morning that she was having second thoughts about going through with the wedding." Frowning, he waved an impatient hand. "Not because she was falling for that Linton character. She wasn't. The gal was too smart for that. She was keeping tabs on him like I asked her to."

He paused to take another sip of his brandy. The light was beginning to fade outside, and Sloan reached to turn on a lamp.

"She was upset that morning," James continued. "She told me that she believed Linton was really falling for her, and that was causing her to have second thoughts about settling for a marriage of convenience. Said maybe the both of you deserved better. I've no doubt she would have come around and done the sensible thing. She always does. But while she was out there on the cliff, someone came up behind her and pushed her over."

I tightened my grip on Sloan's hand.

"Brooke figured that much out this morning," Sloan said. "She climbed down and found Cameron's locket on the ledge."

"Smart gal." He shot me an approving glance. "The ledge saved Cameron's life. But it knocked her out for a while. When she came to, it was dark. She had her cell phone in her pocket and she called me, told me what happened and drove herself back here. We sat right in this very spot and decided what to do next."

"So she drove her car back here and not the would-be killer?" I asked.

"Yes." There was a ruthless light in James's eyes now. "I wanted the bastard to worry and wonder how that car had gotten back here. And whether or not Cameron could still be alive."

"So you let us all believe that she'd gone away to think about the wedding," Sloan said.

James nodded. "Then I waited for someone to show their hand."

"And you didn't think I had a right to know where she was?" Sloan asked. His voice was soft and tight with anger.

When he answered, James's voice was tired. "Cameron didn't see who pushed her. The noise of the sea and the wind blocked any sound. I wasn't about to trust anyone." He met Sloan's eyes steadily. "You'll have to forgive the overprotectiveness of a father."

A tense silence followed.

I took a sip of my brandy to ease the tightness in my throat. "Why L.A.?"

James met my eyes, and I saw regret and something else, something that I'd seen before when he looked at me. Hunger? "She wanted to see you, to be close to you."

"She knew about me?"

"I told her that night when we were deciding what to do. I'd been thinking of getting in touch with you, but it was her idea that I send you that letter. We figured that you'd make an appearance here and that would stir things up."

"The return of the long-lost twin?" I asked around the tight ball that had formed in my throat. "How could you have been so sure I'd take the bait?"

James gave me a steady look. "You have McKenzie genes in you. I knew that curiosity would bring you here. But I wasn't expecting the memory loss story— that was a stroke of genius. I had to move up the wedding to really force the attacker's hand."

There was a knock on the door, and Sloan rose to answer it. The interruption gave me a chance to play James's words over in my mind. "You have McKenzie blood." What I'd suspected but never quite believed had turned out to be true. I was James and Elizabeth's daughter. And my sister was alive.

Elena came in pushing a cart, and for a while the only sound in the room was the clink of china and silver as she set out dinner on James's desk. When she'd lit the candles and pushed the cart out of the room, James said, "Shall we eat?"

I put my brandy snifter down. "I can't. Not until you tell me why you gave me up for adoption."

Sloan returned to his place beside me and took my hand in his. "You're going to have to explain that to me, too."

James kept his eyes steady on mine. "I gave you up for adoption because I loved your mother, and I thought it would save her life. I thought I was in love with my first wife, Sarah, too. But we met in our teens, and during the ten years we were married, we changed, grew up I guess. She wanted something besides ranch life. I wasn't surprised when she ran away. The surprise was that she chose my best friend." He nodded to Sloan. "Your father."

"That must have been hard," I said.

"I told myself that it happens. Lancelot was Arthur's best friend, and Guinevere fell for him. I hoped that they would be happy together."

"They were in love, then?" I asked.

"Why else would they have run off together?"

"You didn't try to find them?"

"Sure." James frowned. "But the P.I. I hired never found a trace."

I gripped Sloan's hand harder. Because we were talking about his father, and it didn't sound as if James had really wanted to find them.

"I was fifty-five when I met Elizabeth Cameron, and it was love at first sight for both of us. I took one look at her and thought this was the woman I was meant to be with. It was the same for her. She'd never wanted to marry, never considered it until she met me. What we shared was a rare and special kind of love—the kind that you experience when you meet the mate that you were created for. If you haven't experienced it, you won't understand what I'm saying."

I thought I knew what he was talking about, but I didn't dare look at Sloan, didn't dare think about it.

"Elizabeth was thirty-five when we married, twenty years my junior. The one bone of contention between us was that I wanted children and she didn't. She didn't want anything else to interfere with her art. In her mind, marriage had interfered enough. But I persisted. I'm not sorry about that. In the end she gave in and agreed to give me one child."

James took another sip of brandy, then set the glass down. "From the beginning of the pregnancy, she was plagued with depression. I took her to the best doctors, and finally we ended up in a clinic in Switzerland where they supposedly had some expertise. But they could do nothing for her. When the doctor told me we were having twins, I didn't dare tell her. I know it sounds unbelievable now, but when the person you love is sick, you become desperate. Your mother's psychological condition was too delicate, too precarious. I was afraid that another baby might push her over the edge."

He drew in a breath and let it out. "That's when I made the hardest decision I've ever made. I brought you back here on a separate plane and arranged for your

adoption through a private agency. I selected your
parents because I recognized in your mother the same
kind of dedication to work that I'd seen in Elizabeth.
And I suppose that giving you to them helped me to live
with the guilt I felt for pressuring Elizabeth into having
you and Cameron."

Odd—there was a part of me that wanted to cry, but
my eyes were as dry as dust. "Did Doc Carter know
about my adoption?"

James met my eyes. "No one knew about it. I handled
it myself. The first person I told about it was your sister."

"And did it work? Did bringing just one baby home
help Elizabeth to get better?"

"Yes. For a while she was fine, back to her old self.
She loved Cameron, and told me more than once that she
was glad I'd pressured her into having a child of our
own. With all the drugs in her system during delivery, she
didn't remember having two babies. I thought everything was going to be fine. Then without warning, her
bouts of depression returned. This time none of the medi-
cations worked. There were times when she couldn't get
out of bed. She couldn't paint. That was what destroyed
her. She felt that she'd lost her art. Then she committed
suicide. Carter said it was postpartum depression. They
were just beginning to recognize it as a disease. But that
doesn't change the fact that by pressuring Elizabeth to
have a child, I killed her and lost you."

There was silence in the room. So many emotions
were pouring through me, and I couldn't help feeling
sorry for the man who was sitting across from me.

Finally James spoke. "Can you ever forgive me?"

I studied him for a moment. "I think you've been

punished enough. You made the best decision that you could, the one that you thought was right. And I have really wonderful parents." But my hand shook as I set down my brandy glass.

Sloan rose and drew me to my feet. "She's tired. I think she's had enough for one night."

James met his eyes. "She shouldn't be alone."

"She won't be."

I followed Sloan to the door before I remembered the other question I needed to ask. I turned back to find James watching me. "My P.I. friend found papers showing that both Cameron and I were adopted. Why?"

"When I sent you the letter, I also took care to plant the other papers. Over the years, I've contributed quite a bit of money to the agency. Partly because they do good work trying to place children in the right families, but also because I thought I might need them to do me a favor someday. So they obliged me. I was afraid that if you knew I was your father and gave you away, you wouldn't come here. And I wouldn't have blamed you."

I went to him then and leaned down to kiss his cheek. "I would have come. I'm a McKenzie. I can't help being curious."

James hugged me then, tight. When he released me he said to Sloan. "You take care of her."

"I will. And we'll talk more in the morning."

Once outside James's suite, Sloan picked me up and began to carry me down the hall. "Your place or mine?"

"Mine's closer," I said.

And it was.

19

SLOAN POCKETED his cell phone. The state police so far had zip. None of the tire prints they'd taken from the two SUVs on the ranch or from Austin's matched the ones they'd found on the cliff. But they'd identified the caliber of the bullet, and they were checking licenses to see who on the ranch might own a gun that would use it. First thing in the morning, they hoped to have answers.

He strode into the bathroom where Brooke lay with her eyes closed in the hot tub. Only her head was visible beneath the sea of bubbles she'd created. Once he'd undressed her and inspected the bruises himself, he'd insisted that she take a long soak to ease the stiffness she was sure to feel in the morning. She was the one who'd insisted on adding bath salts, but he'd lit the candles.

Hannibal was patrolling the edges of the tub, taking an occasional swing at a bubble or two. Whatever his original differences with Brooke, right now it looked to Sloan as if the cat were on guard duty. He knew the feeling. Three times today he'd nearly lost her.

He shifted his gaze back to Brooke. She was here. She was safe. And he was going to keep her that way. The little line on her forehead told him that she wasn't sleeping. She was thinking, worrying. Odd. He'd only known her for what? Less than forty-eight hours, and he already knew that about her.

But then from the moment he'd nearly run her down on the bluff, he'd felt on some deep, instinctive level that he'd known her forever. James had mentioned the same feeling when he'd described how he'd fallen in love with Elizabeth—meeting that one woman you're destined to be with.

It had struck Sloan then that he'd fallen in love with Brooke Ashby. Like Elizabeth, he hadn't been looking for it, hadn't wanted it really. Wasn't that why he'd agreed to go along with the proposition that Cameron and James had presented to him in Kentucky? Marriage with Cameron would have been safe. No emotional risk, no fears of abandonment where she was concerned. She'd never leave him the way his parents had because he and Cameron had both loved the ranch.

Loving Brooke was a different matter. It made him vulnerable. He didn't know how she felt about him. Oh, she wanted him, but she had her life and career in L.A. And while the chemistry between them was strong, it didn't equal love. He'd decided that he didn't want to lose her, but what did she feel? The urge to go to her now, to drag her out of that nest of bubbles and ask her was almost overpowering.

But he couldn't. If nothing else those worry lines stopped him cold. James had given her a lot to think about tonight. She'd been kind to her father, kinder than he might have been. No, he couldn't add to her burden right now. He watched the little line on her forehead deepen. He could imagine what she was feeling. Abandonment. He'd experienced that at an early age. They came from different worlds, yet they had that in common.

And he knew what he could do to make her forget about that, at least for tonight. Moving to the edge of the tub, he sat down. "Stop thinking."

Brooke opened her eyes and met his. "That's difficult advice to follow. I keep going over everything in my mind. That's what I do sometimes when I'm working on a particularly tough plot twist. I'm trying to shift things around, juxtapose them so that I can dream up story lines from all angles."

He dipped a hand beneath the bubbles to test the temperature of the water. "What particular things are you looking at?"

"The timing, for one. I think I understand why the would-be killer chose that particular day to follow Cameron out to the cliff and push her off. The two of you had had a quarrel. If her body had been found, the police would have had two theories to pursue. Suicide or murder. She either followed in her mother's footsteps or you would have been the prime suspect."

His brows shot up.

"It's always the fiancé or the husband the police suspect first. And you did have opportunity. You were at the ranch the entire day. You would have made a great scapegoat."

Leaning over, he ran a finger along her jawline. "What other angles are you looking at?"

"Motives. In all good mysteries the why always leads to the who."

"In this case, we've narrowed the field to the people who were in the barn today and could have sliced your girth."

"True. Beatrice, Marcie and Austin have alibis for the day that Cameron disappeared. That leaves Hal and Doc Carter. Unless they had accomplices. Take Hal. If the why was to make Austin the heir, it wouldn't have worked if he didn't have an airtight alibi. So Austin and Marcie go to Vegas and Hal slips away to push Cameron off the cliff."

Sloan turned the tap on.

"What are you doing that for?"

"The water is cooling. Go ahead and tell me what your plot line is for Beatrice and Doc Carter."

She sighed. "That one is a little less feasible, but I'm thinking it might work on *Secrets*—a torrid affair between Santa Claus and the Snow Queen."

"Come again?"

After explaining her initial impressions of Doc Carter and Beatrice, Brooke went on. "In this one, the why is the same—to get rid of Cameron and make Austin the heir. I imagine that Beatrice might share Cameron's frustration and resentment that the McKenzie men are such patriarchs. If Austin inherits, she has the satisfaction of knowing that the land passes on to her progeny rather than James's."

"The only problem is that Doc Carter was a very happily married man until a year ago, and I have trouble picturing him having a torrid affair with anyone."

"Well, there is that. Not all story lines are equally good. And there's always the possibility that the would-be killer's motives had nothing to do with who inherits the ranch. Maybe it was personal. Maybe someone just wanted Cameron dead."

"Take a break. Time enough to think about it in the

morning." After turning off the water, he lifted the cat off the edge of the tub, carried him through the bedroom, and put him out the door. "The state police hope to have some answers by morning," he continued as he reentered the bathroom. Sloan filled her in on what he'd learned while he sat on the edge of the tub and pulled off his boots.

"There's another plot line that I'm fooling around with, but I haven't been able to come up with anything."

"What's that?"

"Don't laugh. I can't help feeling that there's some connection between the untimely deaths of the previous mistresses of the hacienda and the attacks on Cameron and me."

"Why would you think that?" Sloan asked as he stripped off his shirt.

"Because if I were plotting this as a story line there would have to be a connection. Plus, I don't think it's a coincidence that the mistresses of this house have all...I..."

It gave Sloan a great deal of satisfaction to note the way her sentence trailed off when he stepped out of his jeans.

"You're stripping."

"James is right. You *are* a bright gal." He kept his eyes on hers as he hooked his thumbs in the elastic waistband of his briefs and eased them slowly down over his hips. When they dropped to the floor, he stepped out of them. Her eyes had lowered to his erection, and though he hadn't thought it possible, he grew even harder.

"I want you, Brooke."

Not raising her eyes, she lifted a hand out of the water and beckoned him to join her. "Come in. The water's fine."

He lowered himself into the frothy bubbles so that he

was sitting opposite her, his legs tangled with hers. "Close quarters."

"Very observant."

Sloan scooped up bubbles and tossed them at her. She grinned as she brushed them off her cheek, and he had the satisfaction of seeing that worry line fade from her forehead.

"Would you like some soap?" Without waiting for his answer, she blew a wad of bubbles into his face.

In retaliation, he lifted one of her feet and began to massage the instep.

He heard her breath shudder out. "I'm thinking of a plot line myself." He continued to massage her foot. "But I'm not sure of the technical terms. This is what you might call an opening encounter." He slipped one finger in and out between each of her toes. "Right?"

"Right." Her voice had become breathy, the way it always did when she was aroused. And her eyes—those fascinating green eyes—had darkened.

Slowly, he ran his hand up her calf and traced a pattern on the back of her knee.

She trembled.

"A complication," he said and watched her tremble again. Leaning forward, his gaze never leaving her face, he danced his fingers up her inner thigh. "The tension builds." He could feel it building within himself.

"Sloan, I—" Her voice was a whisper.

"What comes next, Brooke? Tell me." But he didn't wait for her answer before he traced one finger down the slick softness of her fold. "This?"

"Mmmmm." She arched toward where his finger lingered at the entrance to her heat.

"And then?"

"Crisis," she murmured.

He pushed his finger into her, just a little.

"More," she whispered.

"Tell me what comes next?"

"Climax."

He pushed two fingers into her. She arched upward. "Yes."

Water sloshed over the edges of the tub and two candles sputtered as Sloan moved to cover her body with his. He urged her legs apart and entered her.

"We're going to drown," she said as she wrapped her arms around him.

"Practice holding your breath," he said and took her.

IN THE DARKNESS of the gardens, a shadow paced—forward and back, forward and back. She should be dead. She should be dead. She should be dead.

The chant grew louder and louder as the pacing picked up speed. Three times she'd escaped. Three times. It couldn't be tolerated. It wouldn't be tolerated.

Fury boiled up with such force that it seemed to become a separate entity in the surrounding air. The shadow stopped pacing abruptly and turned to face the hacienda.

Breathe in. Breathe out. Control. It had to be regained. It was all-important. Nothing could be accomplished without it.

She should be dead. And she would be dead. Tomorrow. Moonlight fell in a silvery blanket over the sleeping ranch and the shadow's gaze swept the gardens, the land and the hills beyond, gathering in the strength that came from knowing this would never belong to Cameron McKenzie.

When the pacing began again it was slower, more purposeful. Gradually, a plan took root and began to grow.

20

THE SKY WAS STILL the color of pewter when something—a ringing sound—pulled me out of sleep. I managed to get one of my eyes open and discovered I was lying with my head on Sloan's shoulder. He stirred, removing one of the arms he'd wrapped around me, and groped on the bedside table until he located his cell. The ringing stopped.

"Yeah." There was silence for a while. A phone call at this hour couldn't be good. I opened my other eye, but when I tried to pull away, Sloan's other arm, which was still around me, tightened.

"Thanks." He ended the call and turned to me. I didn't like the frown on his face. "That was the state police. They found a vehicle whose tires match the tracks at the cliff."

"Who does it belong to?"

"Doc Carter."

I stared at him trying to process the information. Doc Carter was the last person I would have suspected of shooting down Sloan's plane. I was about to say so when Sloan continued. "The caliber of the bullet they recovered from the plane matches the Winchester rifle they found in the trunk of his car."

"But why? You don't suppose my Snow Queen—Santa Claus theory is for real?"

"They've taken him in for questioning. As soon as they get some answers, we'll know."

"It doesn't make sense."

"He had the opportunity to cut the saddle girth," Sloan pointed out.

"And he didn't have a solid alibi for the day that Cameron disappeared," I recalled. "He thought maybe playing golf."

"The state police may be able to refresh his memory," Sloan said.

But it still didn't make sense to me. Why would Doc Carter want to kill Cameron?

Reading my mind again, Sloan drew me closer and kissed my forehead. "I can't think of a reason why he'd want to harm Cameron, either, but we should have some answers soon."

Sloan's phone rang again. "It's the stables," he said as he took the call.

I could tell from the expression on his face that the news wasn't good. It just never is when someone calls you in the middle of the night. I glanced out the balcony window to see pink streaks in the lightening sky. Or at the crack of dawn.

Sloan got out of bed and walked into the bathroom to gather up his clothes. "That was Gus. He was making his morning rounds and he says there's something wrong with Saturn. He can't wake him up."

I threw back the covers. "I'll come with you."

"No." He'd already dragged on jeans when he came back to the bed. "The threat to you may be over, but we're not taking any chances. You'll stay here. Give me your cell phone."

When he handed it to me, he picked up my cell and started pressing in numbers. "I'm going to put my cell number on speed dial. If you need me, if anything at all happens, just press one."

He passed me back the phone and then met my eyes directly. "You're not to leave this room. Give me your word."

"Okay."

By the time he'd finished dressing, I'd pulled on my own jeans and a T-shirt and fastened my cell to my belt. My masquerade was about to end, and when it did, I wanted to be in my own clothes.

I followed Sloan to the door. As he stepped outside, he said, "Lock it and don't leave here until I come back."

"I gave you my word."

He leaned down to kiss me once—hard. I closed the door, locked it and then went to the window. In less than a minute, I saw him going down the path to the stable at a run. If Doc Carter confessed, this might be the last time I stood here looking out at the ranch from Cameron's point of view.

But it wasn't going to be the last night I spent with Sloan. The one thing that we hadn't done during the night was talk about what was going to happen once we figured out who was trying to kill Cameron and she was able to return. Lots of things were still up in the air. But I was not going to let Sloan Campbell walk out of my life. Walking around in my sister's clothes and living her life for a few days had at least done that much for me. I was going to fight for what I wanted.

I frowned. Right now, I needed to think. I just wasn't convinced that Doc Carter was the villain of this particular scenario. Turning around, I began to pace the length of the room. I couldn't get it out of my mind that the attempts on Cameron's life and mine were somehow connected to the deaths or disappearances of the other mistresses of the Montega Hacienda. But if I couldn't come up with a reason for Doc Carter wanting Cameron dead, how was I going to come up with one for him wanting my mother dead?

Even if he had a partner, who would it be? What was the motive? With a sigh, I sank down on the foot of the bed. I wasn't accomplishing anything except making my headache come back. Maybe the problem was that I was a writer. If this were a story line on *Secrets*, of course I'd want to connect my sister's disappearance to the other mysteries of the hacienda. But real life was never as neat as fiction.

What I needed was coffee. I frowned realizing that I wasn't going to get any until Sloan came back. It was then that I heard Hannibal's meow. I glanced around the room, then remembered that Sloan had put him out last night.

Hannibal meowed again in a very annoyed tone and I crossed to the door and opened it.

Hannibal was there all right. So was Beatrice and she had a gun in her hand.

"I'll shoot you," she said in a voice she might use to discuss the weather.

The look in her eyes told me that she would.

She gestured with the gun to the right. "Come."

With Hannibal walking beside me, I moved down the hall.

"Where are we going?" I asked. But I knew. My body knew, too. Fear was already a hard, icy ball in my stomach. I couldn't let it spread. I needed a clear head.

"If you're hoping to be rescued, you won't be," Beatrice continued in a mild tone. "The drug I gave Saturn will keep Sloan's mind occupied for a while. I doubt he'll give you even a thought until the vet arrives and figures out what's wrong."

She'd drugged the horse. I felt a flare of anger, welcomed it. Think, I told myself. You just need a plan. What would Mallory Carstairs do in a scene like this? What would Cameron do?

"Don't think of running," Beatrice said just as that scenario flashed into my mind.

So much for Plan A, and Plan B hadn't come to me by the time we reached the door to the bell tower. I walked on past, but Beatrice said, "Stop."

Behind me, I heard her unlock the door and push it open.

"After you."

Hannibal followed me into the tower. The moment I looked at the stairs spiraling upward, a wave of dizziness hit me. The cat had no such problem. He'd already disappeared around the first curve. Feeling nauseated, I slumped against the wall for support. When I felt my cell phone press into my hip, I remembered that Sloan had programmed his number into it.

"Take a deep breath," Beatrice said.

"Give me a minute." I didn't have to fake the fear in my voice, and I prayed she wouldn't see my hand go to my cell. In my mind, I pictured the buttons and prayed again that I was pressing number one and then Send.

The gun poked into my spine.

"I really can't do this. You know what happened the last time we were in the tower."

"Yes. You nearly fell. I was so tempted to just give you that little push that you needed. But there would have been too many witnesses."

I sagged farther against the wall. "Beatrice, I can't."

"Yes, you can." Her voice was soft and soothing just as it had been the other time, and it made my skin crawl. She didn't take my hand this time. Instead, she pressed the gun harder against my spine. "A bullet will hurt. That's what I told your mother. If you hadn't come back, we could have avoided this. Now, you'll have to go up there just like Elizabeth did."

At the mention of Elizabeth's name, my mind cleared and become suddenly calm. But I kept my steps tentative and leaned heavily against the wall as I climbed. "You killed my mother, didn't you?"

"It was so easy," Beatrice said. "She was doing so well, and then her depression came back. The doctors couldn't explain it. But I could. I'd replaced her medication with simple vitamins, and no one suspected a thing. When they tried a new drug, I just replaced that one, too. No one was the wiser. Men are such fools. Everyone accepted the fact that she climbed up here one night and followed in the footsteps of the first mistress of the hacienda."

"What actually happened?" I asked.

"She was having trouble sleeping and she would go down to the kitchen to warm milk for herself. One night I joined her and slipped a drug into the drink. Then all I had to do was to help her up the stairs just as I'm helping you."

We'd rounded the first curve of the stairs, and I could see the opening to the bell tower above me. Another wave of dizziness struck and I shoved it down. I wasn't going to think about how my mother had fallen out of the tower. Instead, I was going to keep Beatrice talking so that Sloan would know where we were.

SATURN LAY ON HIS SIDE, his eyes open but glazed. Sloan dropped to his knees next to Gus and ran a hand down the horse's neck.

"He looks drugged."

"That would be my guess. Vet should be here at any minute. Called him before I called you."

"Good," Sloan said as he continued to frown at the horse. "Good."

For a moment they sat in silence, both trying to comfort Saturn as best they could.

"Who?" Sloan asked the question out loud, but Gus didn't answer. He didn't have an answer himself. But he was going to find out.

When his cell rang, he lifted it automatically and put it to his ear. "Yeah?"

The voice that he heard coming through the line turned his blood to ice.

"...know what happened the last time we were in the tower."

"Yes. You nearly fell. I was so tempted to just give you that little push that you needed. But there would have been too many witnesses."

Sloan was already out of the stall and running when he yelled back to Gus. "Beatrice has got Brooke. She's going to push her out of the tower."

I DREW IN A DEEP BREATH as I stepped into the small space of the tower. Now that we were here, I was trapped. Any step I took brought me to the edge of the low wall. I pushed the thought out of my mind, and gazed at the landscapes my mother had painted. In the east, the sun had risen halfway on the horizon. I recalled the painting in the dining room of just this scene.

"It won't be long now." Beatrice's voice held a note of promise.

Even as a chill moved up my spine, I turned to the left and looked at the stables and the flat range beyond—another scene my mother had painted. I recalled seeing it in the main parlor.

I was not going to follow in the footsteps of the mistresses of the hacienda, I promised myself as I turned to face her. "How did you get away from the flower show on the day I disappeared?"

"I drove there early and made sure that I was seen setting up my display. Then I told the women in the booths next to mine that I had to slip away for a bit to practice my luncheon speech. It didn't take long to drive out to the cliffs, and you were there waiting for me."

"What about yesterday?"

"I went out the back of the greenhouse, walked over to Doc Carter's and borrowed his car and his rifle. He's a creature of habit just as I am, and he spends all his mornings practicing his tee shots on that green he's had landscaped into his backyard. Just as he did on the day you disappeared. I borrowed his car that day, too." She gestured with the gun. "It's time now, Cameron. Turn around."

I held up a hand. "One more question." Out of the corner of my eye, I could see Hannibal walking back and forth like a sentinel on the wall. "What happened to James's first wife?" The merest hint of surprise moved into those cold eyes.

"You know about her?" Beatrice asked.

"You killed her, too, didn't you?"

"She was weak and not worthy of being a mistress here. None of them were. Only the strong survive," Beatrice said. "Sarah was unhappy, restless, and she used to get up in the middle of the night and take walks in the gardens. So predictable. I met her there one night, offered her some sleeping pills, and then all I had to do was wait until she was drowsy. Then I was going to bring her here. She should have died here."

For the first time I heard rage in her voice, and I saw her knuckles whiten on the hand that held the gun. My throat went dry. "Where did she die?"

"In the garden. Sloan's father came along. He saw me, saw the gun. I had to shoot him. Then I shot her and buried them both near the greenhouse."

"And you let everyone believe that they'd run away together?"

"I made them believe it. I packed some clothes for each of them. Then I wrote the note. I'd practiced her handwriting for months. Of course, it was supposed to be for a suicide note. No matter. It was so easy to kill them both. It always is."

Easy to kill people? The horror of what she was saying washed over me, but I couldn't let it affect me. Not yet. Out of the corner of my eye, I saw Sloan running up the path toward the hacienda. I had to keep her talking and focused on me. "Why, Beatrice? Why did you kill them?"

The look she gave me held the first hint of madness

that I'd seen—and the second hint of rage that I'd glimpsed beneath that cold facade. "Because I'm the mistress here. This place should have been at least half mine. James inherited only because he was a man. Our father never believed that a woman could run the place. But I can. I have. I will always be the mistress here."

"So that's why you pushed me off the cliff that day."

She blinked. "Yes." I heard true emotion in her voice. "History was repeating itself, but in reverse. James should have left half the estate to Austin. I bore my son for that very purpose, knowing that one day he would inherit and I would have what was mine. Then James decided to leave the place to you and to Sloan Campbell—a man who isn't even a McKenzie."

In a way, in spite of what she'd done, I could sympathize with the injustice that had been done to her.

Beatrice drew in a deep breath. "But you came back. You shouldn't have come back. I warned you in that phone call." She took a step toward me. "You should have taken my warning and gone away."

She was close now, so close that I could reach out and touch the gun. Her eyes were calm again, and very cold. The ice queen.

"You can go by yourself or I can shoot you," she said in that soothing voice.

SLOAN WAS PRAYING as he took the stairs two at a time, then raced down the corridor to the open door of the bell tower. He stopped then. He'd seen the two of them just before he'd reached the house. The image would be forever burned on his brain—Brooke standing with her back to the low wall, and Beatrice with a gun in her hand.

The sick ball of fear had settled in his stomach then. He wasn't going to reach them in time. And even if he did storm up those stairs, Beatrice would hear him coming. All she had to do was squeeze the trigger.

He took a step forward and saw the rope to the bell. Taking it into his hands, he prayed that it would work.

"I'LL JUMP BY MYSELF." I'd said the words, but I couldn't seem to move. In a minute, she was going to pull that trigger. It was all I could think of, and yet I couldn't unfreeze.

The bell clanged—so loud that I could feel the vibrations on my skin. The noise shocked me out of my paralysis. Beatrice started, too. I prayed that my reflexes were faster as I dived at her, grabbing her gun hand with both of mine and shoving hard.

The gun went flying out of the tower. We both lost our footing and fell on the wall. For a moment we lay balanced precariously on it—teetering—I with the stones pressing into my back and Beatrice on top of me. I was sure that we were both going to go over.

Then she pulled herself off me and backed up several steps until she was against the opposite wall. I was still struggling for balance when she started toward me again. Then Hannibal leaped. He hit Beatrice midchest, and I heard her scream as she stumbled backward, hit the wall and toppled over.

Digging my fingers into the edge of the wall, I managed to get my balance. Then I had to sit down. Sloan found me on the floor of the bell tower with Hannibal on my lap when he burst through the door. He didn't say a word. He just pulled Hannibal and me onto his lap.

We sat there for a long time.

21

WHEN THE STATE TROOPER, Lieutenant Brady, finally closed his notebook, Sloan rose. It was nearly noon, and he hadn't had a break since the police had arrived on the scene and set up shop in the main parlor. He glanced down the length of the room to where Brooke was still being questioned by a female trooper. He'd been the one who'd insisted that the police use the parlor because he hadn't wanted to let Brooke out of his sight. Evidently Hannibal felt the same way because the cat hadn't left her side since they'd come down from the bell tower.

It would be a long time before he could get the image out of his mind of Beatrice holding that gun on her and knowing that he wasn't going to make it in time. And he didn't think he'd ever be rid of the sound of Beatrice screaming as she fell. He hadn't reached the tower yet, and for those last few endless steps, he'd thought it had been Brooke who'd fallen. Even when he'd seen her sitting there with the cat, he hadn't believed it. He'd had to touch her, hold her. And then he'd listened as she'd poured out everything Beatrice told her. When he'd learned that his father hadn't abandoned him, Sloan couldn't sort through the flood of feelings that moved through him. He'd simply held on to Brooke. It hadn't been until the troopers had finally climbed the stairs that either one of them had moved.

Since then, he hadn't had a chance to talk with her or with James for that matter. They'd all been caught up in a seemingly endless round of interrogations. As far as he knew, Austin and the Lintons were still being questioned in the kitchen wing. And he'd been told that the troopers had talked to James in his suite.

"How long before you'll be through with Ms. Ashby?" Sloan asked.

"Hard to say. We're taking her over her statement on what exactly happened in the tower in those last few minutes."

"She's told you what happened." Impatience swirled through him. And anger. Ever since the fear and the shock and the relief had faded, a fury had been building inside of him.

"There are things that Beatrice Caulfield told her that we have to follow up on." Brady spoke in a mild tone. "We'd like to make sure Ms. Caulfield didn't have an accomplice."

Sloan frowned. "You think her son may have been in on it with her? Or Doc Carter?"

"Not necessarily. We're just trying to eliminate those possibilities." Brady's tone was mild. "There were a lot of people who might have wanted to eliminate Cameron McKenzie. It's unfortunate that no one chose to report the attack on her five weeks ago."

"Yes, it is, isn't it?" Sloan murmured.

Brady glanced at his watch. "We may be able to wrap it up in another half hour or so."

Satisfied that Brooke would be busy for a while yet, Sloan said, "I'll be back." Then he left the room and strode down the corridor to James's suite. He wanted to check on the old man, and there were things he needed to say to him.

Sloan entered the room without knocking. James was sitting in his massive chair. Only this time he wasn't behind his desk. The old man had moved the chair and angled it so that he was staring out at his domain—the stables and the land beyond.

James turned. "How is she?"

Sloan strode forward. "She's fine—or at least she will be. But it's no thanks to you. You sat there on that throne of yours, pulling strings the way you always do. Hiding Cameron away and luring into your game a daughter you'd never met. You damn near got her killed."

"Yes. Yes, I did."

Damn him. The old man's simple admission had more of his anger fading, but Sloan wasn't finished. "Why? Why couldn't you have just told the police when Cameron was attacked? Why this elaborate charade?"

James leaned forward then. "Do you think the police would have found the truth? Do you think they could have kept Cameron safe from another attack?"

Knowing what they knew now about Beatrice, Sloan had to admit he had a point.

Shaking his head, James sighed. "I decided to bring Brooke here because I thought her appearance on the scene would stir things up and bring everything to a head. I never expected that she would come here impersonating Cameron. And I never dreamed that Beatrice would... My God, I never suspected that my sister was capable of…" James raised a hand and dropped it. "She murdered three times. She murdered my wife, Sarah, and your father—a man who was my best friend. Then she murdered Elizabeth. And for what?"

Sloan narrowed his eyes. His anger still hadn't run its course, but the look in James's eyes, a mixture of shock and sorrow, had him banking it. He put out his hand and gripped James's arm. "From what Brooke has told me, she murdered three times because she felt she had a right to inherit at least half of this estate, and the only reason why she wasn't allowed to was because she wasn't a man. You might want to give that some thought before you perpetuate the problem."

James's chin lifted. "What are you saying?"

"You know exactly what I'm saying. You manipulated Cameron into marrying me in order to get half her inheritance. I don't imagine she's any happier with that than Beatrice was when she didn't inherit anything."

James rose from his chair. "If you're saying that Cameron, that a daughter of mine would turn into a crazed killer…"

Sloan's brows rose. "Don't you dare twist my words, old man. I'm not saying that at all. I'm merely saying that you'd better think long and hard about what you're doing with your kingdom. And remember, you've got a second daughter who isn't nearly as predictable as Cameron."

"True."

To Sloan's astonishment, James smiled, then broke into a loud bellowing laugh that filled the room. He stared as James lowered himself back into his chair. When he finally stopped laughing, James said, "Cameron said much the same thing to me on the phone a few moments ago." He dug a slip of paper out of his pocket and handed it to Sloan. "She wants to talk to you."

Sloan glanced down at the paper and then back at James. "I'm not going to marry her."

Something came into James's eyes then, something Sloan couldn't quite read.

"I figured that."

A suspicion formed in the back of Sloan's mind but before he could give voice to it, James said, "Go ahead and call Cameron. If it makes you feel any better, she's already told me she's not marrying you, either. And she's in perfect agreement with you on how much blame I should be shouldering for all of this."

Reaching for his cell phone, Sloan moved through one of the open doors to the patio outside of James's suite, then punched in the number.

When she picked up the call, Cameron said, "I hear you've had a rough time."

"Rough time?" Sloan repeated. He hadn't quite put together in his mind what he wanted to say to Cameron. "I guess you could say so."

She laughed softly. "You're pissed at Dad and me both, aren't you?"

He nearly smiled then, and was surprised that he could. But then Cameron had always understood him so well. Just as he had always understood her. "To borrow a phrase from James, you're a smart gal. It was a near thing." He paused to push the memory out of his mind. "We nearly lost your sister."

"Yeah. I got that much from Dad. Believe me, we had no idea that Beatrice was the one who pushed me. My prime suspect was Austin, but I didn't think he had the guts to do it himself."

"The police are still checking to make sure he wasn't involved in some way, but I think they'll find that Beatrice was acting alone, albeit perhaps in some measure on his behalf."

"What's my sister like?"

"Like?" Sloan let his gaze move out past the gardens to the stables and the hills beyond. A series of scenes moved through his mind—nearly running her down on the bluff, kissing her in the garden, watching her stand up to James at that dinner party, finding her poking around in his refrigerator, seeing her face down Beatrice in the tower. He wondered when it was that he'd first started falling in love with her.

"Earth to Sloan," Cameron prompted.

Sloan tried to clear his mind. "Your sister, Brooke, is curious and stubborn and courageous and…amazing. And I'm in love with her, Cam."

When Cameron spoke, he could hear the smile in her voice. "I take it our engagement's off."

He smiled then. "Yeah. I'd say so. It'll piss the old man off."

"Not at all. Haven't you figured it out yet? Part of the reason he contacted Brooke was he thought the two of you might make a better match than you and I. I told him the night I left for L.A. that I was having second thoughts about marrying you. I told him that both of us deserved the chance to find what he'd found with Elizabeth."

Sloan turned and saw that James was watching him. He should have guessed it sooner. "That sly old fox."

"Oh, he's that all right, and we just continue to play

into his hands. But in this case, I think he's done us both a favor. After watching my sister's soap for five weeks, I think she just might be perfect for you. You'll never be able to predict what she'll do next."

"Well, there's that." Then his expression sobered. "But that night when you left, you weren't going to go along with the old man's plans, were you? I've had some time to think about it. You were really going to call off the wedding."

Cameron laughed. "We'll never know that for sure, will we? Why don't we just say that I'm happy to have a twin who can take my place. She is going to take my place, right?"

"I haven't gotten her input on that yet."

"Want some advice from a kid sister?"

"Yeah." It was his turn to laugh now, and he felt his tension and anger melt away. "Yeah, that would be good."

WHEN SLOAN AND SATURN found me, I was sitting on the bluff very close to the spot where I'd first met Sloan. He didn't say a word as he dismounted. After he'd secured the horse, he sat down next to me and merely put his arm around me. Almost at once, the thoughts that had been swirling around in my head settled, and I felt suddenly and completely at home.

"I know you needed some time to think," Sloan said. "But I couldn't give you any more."

"It's all so sad. I'm a writer. I should at least in my imagination be able to understand Beatrice's motivations, but I'm having trouble getting my mind around what she did, what she lived with all of these years."

"She did it for what we're looking at right now. But

she can't have been completely sane to have murdered all of them. My father, both of James's wives." His arm tightened around me. "Then to have almost murdered you and Cameron…"

He turned to me then and tipped my face up so that I met his eyes. "I had a talk with Cameron."

My stomach knotted. I didn't want to ask the question, but I had to know the answer. "Did you work everything out?"

"Yeah. You might say that. When do you have to go back to L.A.?"

My heart sank. Did he think that I was just going to leave, that everything that had happened between us was… Another thought occurred to me. Were he and Cameron going to go ahead with their wedding? Had he come up here to say goodbye? "I—" There was a lump in my throat I couldn't seem to get any more words around.

"I want to go with you."

I blinked and stared at him. "You want to go with me?"

"Yeah. To L.A. I've got this little plot—you'd probably call it a story line—and I thought that you might help me flesh it out and then see if it would fly on *Secrets*?"

I studied him, trying to read something in those dark gray eyes. "You have a story line for *Secrets*?"

"Yeah." Sloan tucked a piece of hair behind my ear. "It's about these twins who were separated at birth, and one of them was given up for adoption. Years later, the twin who wasn't given up for adoption disappears just before her wedding, and the other one, just learning of her sister's existence, decides to take her place."

His hand had moved to the back of my neck and those fingers began to work their magic on me. The chill I'd experienced when he'd told me he'd worked things out with Cameron was fading as the heat spread from his touch all the way through me.

"Then there's what you call a complication." He brushed his mouth against mine, and even as he drew back, my lips parted in response.

"A complication?"

"Umm, hmm," he murmured as he leaned down to kiss me lightly again. "She finds that she's very attracted to her twin sister's fiancé."

He was trailing kisses along the side of my jaw. When he reached my ear, he said, "And another complication is that he's incredibly attracted to her. He can't be near her and not want his hands on her. Not want to be inside of her. And that's not all...."

His teeth nipped my earlobe, but then he drew away again. "The final complication is...I love you, Brooke Ashby. I'm not going to marry Cameron. She doesn't want to marry me, either."

For a moment, I didn't know what to say. My blood was pounding and there was a ringing in my ears. This was exactly the way I would have written it—if I were writing it. But this was actually happening to me—Ms. Nothing-ever-happens-to-me Brooke Ashby. Then I saw something come into his eyes. Was it fear?

"You're going to have to say something, Red."

"It's a great story line. But there are so many possible complications. There's the land and James...my father."

"Forget him. He's probably hatching some new plot even as we speak. You come by your talents naturally."

"There's my job in L.A."

"It's not a long commute."

"But—if the wedding's off—I mean—won't my father change the will? Won't you have to make new plans?"

Now it was impatience that flashed in his eyes. "I told you my plans. I'm coming to L.A. for a while. I want us to have some time together away from here. Away from all that's happened here. Gus can run things for a bit. And after James decides what to do with the ranch, we'll come up with a new plan." He tightened his hand at the back of my neck. "Haven't you ever worked with another writer?"

"Collaborated, you mean?"

"Yeah. We can collaborate. There's only one thing you have to say if you want our story line to continue. Don't make me wait any longer to hear it."

Suddenly, I couldn't wait to hear it, either. "I love you, Sloan Campbell."

When his mouth took mine, suddenly all the complications melted away. I knew that we could work everything out. And we would work everything out—together.

Epilogue

I SAT ON THE BED with Hannibal and watched my sister step out of her shoes and then move quickly to the sitting area of her bedroom. My sister. It had been nearly a week since she'd returned to the ranch from Los Angeles, and I was still getting to know her. Still getting used to the idea that she was my sister and that looking at her was like looking into a mirror.

Not that we'd had much chance to really talk to each other yet. The past few days had been hectic. First there'd been more visits from the police, then Beatrice's funeral and finally, my parents had surprised me by flying in from Chicago to assure themselves that I was safe and to meet James. As a result, Cameron and I hadn't been able to spend much time together. Tomorrow we had a date to go riding. Sloan had offered to let me take Saturn, and Cameron would ride Lace Ribbons.

But first we had to get through tonight. An hour ago, right after we'd had dinner, my father—I was still getting used to calling James that—had announced that he'd signed a new will that afternoon, and then he'd revealed the contents. My stomach was still churning, and I was sure that Cameron's was, too. She couldn't be happy with what her father had done.

I'd objected, but neither Sloan nor Cameron had backed me up. However, as soon as James had retired for the night, she'd asked me to come to her room for a sister-to-sister chat.

Cameron flipped on the CD player, and the soft strains of a Chopin étude filled the room. Then she squatted down, opened the small cabinet next to the sofa and grabbed the bag of cat tidbits. The casual way she tossed a handful of them in Hannibal's direction told me that this was part of their nightly routine. When she reached into the cabinet again, I expected her to bring out chocolate, but instead, she withdrew a crystal decanter and two glasses. "I need some brandy," she announced. "How about you?"

"That would be great." Brandy might be just the ticket to settle the nerves that were dancing in my stomach. As she poured us generous amounts, I moved to join her in the small alcove, then took the glass she handed me. We both took a sip before Cameron settled herself in one corner of the sofa, tucked her feet under her and pointed at the other corner.

"Sit," she said. "I told Sloan I wasn't going to send you off to the carriage house until we'd hashed out this business of the will."

I found myself wanting to smile as I sat down. In the short time that I'd known Cameron, I was learning that she had a habit of ordering people around.

"You're upset with Dad because he's leaving a third of the ranch to you."

She also had a remarkable knack for cutting right to the chase. "Aren't you?" I asked. "And Sloan must be, too. I mean, he came back here to marry you and he was counting on inheriting half. Now he only gets a third. And you—" I gestured with the brandy snifter "—you were supposed to inherit half, too. It's not fair."

"Okay, let's talk about fair. In order to get half of the ranch, Sloan and I had to agree to marry and eventually produce a McKenzie heir. Don't get me wrong. I like Sloan, and there's no one I would trust more with half of this ranch, but we were never in love. If we'd gone through with the wedding, we would have had to give up what you and Sloan have found together. Would you want us to have missed out on that?"

"No. Of course not. But what about Austin? He's lost so much. Is it fair that he doesn't inherit anything?"

Cameron's eyes hardened a bit, and I could see James in her. "Austin has to get himself straightened out first. Marcie's been a good influence on him, but he was at the gambling tables in Vegas on the very day that I disappeared. We'll assure him that he has a job here and a chance to prove himself. Don't you think that's fair enough?"

I nodded. I'd had a chance to talk with both Austin and Marcie at Beatrice's funeral, and I believed that with Marcie's help, Austin had a good chance of really turning his life around. "But I still don't think the will is fair to you and Sloan."

"Would you feel better about the will if you'd been raised here?" She made a sweeping gesture with her free hand. "If all this had been a part of your life?"

I frowned as I thought about it. "I suppose."

"Then is it fair that by a twist of fate I grew up here and you were put up for adoption?"

I stared at her. "Okay, maybe you have a point there,

but the fact remains that I wasn't raised here. I don't know anything about breeding or training horses or running a ranch."

"So what? Sloan tells me that you love horses, that you've always dreamed of owning one of your own. And from what I learned watching that soap you write for, you have a quick mind and a fertile imagination. I don't think it will take you long to get up to speed."

I was learning that my sister had a quick mind, too. Not to mention the fact that she would have given Pepper and me a run for our money on the debate team. I took another sip of brandy. "You've been watching *Secrets*?"

She grinned at me. "Every day for the past five weeks—ever since Dad told me about you. I insisted that we couldn't contact you personally. It had to be your decision to come to the ranch. Once he sent the anonymous letter, I made him swear that he wouldn't interfere any more than that."

I studied her. "Why not?"

For the first time, I saw temper flash into her eyes. "Because of what he did to you—putting you up for adoption. It sucks. I think he ought to be horsewhipped."

For the first time since James had revealed the contents of his will—no, for the first time since I'd learned that I had a twin sister, I felt all of my tension ease.

Cameron set her glass down, rose and began to pace back and forth in front of the sofa. "Don't get me wrong. I love Dad, but I can't understand how he could have done that. He gave you up for adoption! He kept us apart all of these years. I simply can't fathom it." She turned to me. "Leaving you a third of the ranch is the least he can do. Sloan and I told him that. We told him that if he didn't leave part of the ranch to you, he'd never see either of us again."

Shock streamed through me. I could see the truth of what she was saying in her eyes, hear it in her voice, and I couldn't even begin to name the emotions swirling through me. Words didn't have a chance of getting past the lump in my throat. Rising, I went to her, put my arms around her and held on tight. After a long moment, I pulled back. "I don't know what to say."

She took my hands and squeezed them. "Tell me that you'll stay here, be my sister and help Sloan and me run this ranch."

Suddenly, it was so simple. "Okay. Okay, I'll do that."

"Fine." Cameron swiped the heels of her hands over the dampness on her cheeks. "Now, I have two more questions."

My brows shot up. "Only two?"

She laughed as we retrieved our brandies. "Two for starters."

"Hey, Red!" We both moved toward the balcony at the sound of Sloan's voice. He was standing below us in the garden, his hands on his hips and a wide smile on his face. I was almost getting used to my heart turning over when I looked at him. Almost.

"You can't have her back yet," Cameron said.

He frowned up at Cameron. "You haven't convinced her to accept the will yet?"

She laughed. "Oh, ye of little faith. Of course, I did. And I didn't even have to pull out my best argument."

"What was it?" I asked curiously.

She made a sweeping gesture with her hand. "The fact that what this hacienda has needed all along is two mistresses. Starting with us, they're all going to lead long, happy lives."

Sloan shifted his gaze to me. "You okay?"

"Yes. I'm fine." And I knew that I was, that somehow everything was finally as it should be.

"Then why don't you stay there with your sister? Get to know one another a little better. I'll see you in the morning."

"I'd like that," I said. But I had second thoughts as soon as he turned and walked toward the carriage house.

"You can always sneak away before morning and surprise him," Cameron said, reading my mind. When he was out of sight, she drew me back into the room. "Now for my first question—what is going to happen to Mallory Carstairs when she comes out of that coma?"

I grinned at her. "She'll be suffering from temporary amnesia, and then, of course, she's going to find out that she has an identical twin sister that she was separated from at birth."

Hannibal glared at us both as we collapsed on the sofa in laughter.

* * * * *

New York Times *bestselling author*
Linda Lael Miller
is back with a new romance
featuring the heartwarming McKettrick family
from Silhouette Special Edition.

SIERRA'S HOMECOMING
by Linda Lael Miller

On sale December 2006,
wherever books are sold.

Turn the page for a sneak preview!

Soft, smoky music poured into the room.

The next thing she knew, Sierra was in Travis's arms, close against that chest she'd admired earlier, and they were slow dancing.

Why didn't she pull away?

"Relax," he said. His breath was warm in her hair.

She giggled, more nervous than amused. What was the matter with her? She was attracted to Travis, had been from the first, and he was clearly attracted to her. They were both adults. Why not enjoy a little slow dancing in a ranch-house kitchen?

Because slow dancing led to other things. She took a step back and felt the counter flush against her lower back. Travis naturally came with her, since they were holding hands and he had one arm around her waist.

Simple physics.

Then he kissed her.

Physics again—this time, not so simple.

"Yikes," she said, when their mouths parted.

He grinned. "Nobody's ever said that after I kissed them."

She felt the heat and substance of his body pressed against hers. "It's going to happen, isn't it?" she heard herself whisper.

"Yep," Travis answered.

"But not tonight," Sierra said on a sigh.

"Probably not," Travis agreed.

"When, then?"

He chuckled, gave her a slow, nibbling kiss. "Tomorrow morning," he said. "After you drop Liam off at school."

"Isn't that…a little…soon?"

"Not soon enough," Travis answered, his voice husky. "Not nearly soon enough."

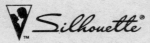

Silhouette®

Romantic
SUSPENSE

INTIMATE MOMENTS™

From *New York Times* bestselling author Maggie Shayne

When Selene comes to the aid of an unconscious stranger, she doesn't expect to be accused of harming him. The handsome stranger's amnesia doesn't help her cause either. Determined to find out what really happened to Cory, the two end up on an intense ride of dangerous pasts and the search for a ruthless killer.

DANGEROUS LOVER #1443
December 2006

Available wherever you buy books.

REQUEST YOUR FREE BOOKS!

2 FREE NOVELS PLUS 2 FREE GIFTS!

HARLEQUIN®

Blaze®

Red-hot reads!

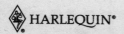

HARLEQUIN®

American R O M A N C E®

IS PROUD TO PRESENT

COWBOY VET
by Pamela Britton

Jessie Monroe is the last person on earth
Rand Sheppard wants to rely on, but he needs
a veterinary technician—yesterday—and she's the
only one for hire. It turns out the woman who
destroyed his cousin's life isn't who Rand thought
she was. And now she's all he can think about!

"Pamela Britton writes the kind of
wonderfully romantic, sexy, witty romance
that readers dream of discovering
when they go into a bookstore."

—*New York Times* bestselling author
Jayne Ann Krentz

*Cowboy Vet is available from
Harlequin American Romance in December 2006.*

www.eHarlequin.com   HARPBDEC

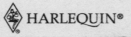